Passions of the Wolf

Passions of the Wolf

Beth Murray

Winchester, UK
Washington, USA

First published by Lodestone Books, 2016
Lodestone Books is an imprint of John Hunt Publishing Ltd., Laurel House, Station Approach,
Alresford, Hants, SO24 9JH, UK
office1@jhpbooks.net
www.johnhuntpublishing.com

For distributor details and how to order please visit the 'Ordering' section on our website.

ISBN: 978 1 78535 028 3
Library of Congress Control Number: 2015930437

A CIP catalogue record for this book is available from the British Library.

Design: Stuart Davies

Printed in the USA by Edwards Brothers Malloy

Dedicated to Kaitlin, Chris, and Charlotte,
My fantastically strange family,
with love, always.

Prologue

It wasn't real. None of it was real. The blood seeped across the kitchen floor, creating tiny streams in the grooves in between the otherwise clean white tiles. The colour of it wasn't real, was too dark and too dull to her eyes. The smell of it wasn't real, was too much like copper in the back of her throat. Yet the smell and taste, like the colour, was just too faded to her senses. She had switched the radio, which stood in the far side of the kitchen, on loud but the faint sound of music could have been travelling to her over miles. Even the pain that should have been tearing at her wrists, from where the blood still steadily flowed was almost unnoticeable. There was nothing that any of her senses presented to her that felt true.

She lay there on the cold tiles of the kitchen floor, watching the red rivers of her life run further away from her, and felt nothing. Numbness had spread throughout her entire body and had consumed her soul. The dream-like world that was her life was ending, but the thought brought neither happiness nor regret – the knowledge was simply there. And it was the numbness that she had sought, her quest for the pain and sadness to end that had led her to pick up the knife. It was for the inability to feel anything that had caused her to place the blade, tentatively at first, against her left wrist. And to then force it deeper, opening her arm from the wrist to elbow, to watch as her flesh opened willingly to the metal. Her right arm had posed more problems, the treacherous left hand shaking and weak, but it eventually also welcomed the blade. Then, knowing that its job was done, the knife dropped serenely to the floor, small droplets of blood bouncing down around it like rain.

Miles away, that radio still played while she simply lay and watched her blood move further and further away, her mind for once untroubled and free of the aching pain that had set the events in motion. She closed her eyes and waited, waited for the numbness to totally consume her; for the debilitating ticking of her heart to finally fall quiet.

In her self-imposed darkness that was growing steadily, blissfully, darker, she heard the faint music of the song stop, to be replaced by the faint sounds of the DJ talking, the words at first indistinguishable. She squeezed her eyes shut tighter, her forehead creasing, as the words being spoken began to grow louder, the distance between her and the radio closing. Soon the words were no longer indistinguishable; were beginning to get through the black fog that had filled her mind, and started to boom noisily in her ears.

"…next dedication is from an anonymous listener. The message says, 'This song is for all of those who are hurting and feeling pain. Hold on.' Here is REM's 'Everybody Hurts' ."

Shock and wonder slashed through her euphoric emptiness as he spoke. It was for her; the dedication was for *her*, she was sure of it! If it hadn't been, if those apt words had not been meant for her to hear, then why had they reached her? Why did *they* feel real when nothing else did?

As the introduction to the song started to sound in her head, she fought against the oncoming rush of reality, the futility of her efforts only causing the fog to be driven away quicker. She was growing aware of what lay behind the thinning veil of her own defeat; could feel the coolness of the tiles beneath her body; could feel the strands of light brown hair that lay across her cheek; could smell her blood that was pooled beside her; could feel the swelling ache of the cuts that she had made.

She opened her eyes, the brightness of the room exploding in her mind. Looking at the white tiles before her was like looking into the core of the sun, the blood that had escaped her blazing like fire. Everything imbued with radiance and brilliance. Even as a part of her yearned for the darkness, again the intensity of the newly discovered world around her, held her captivated.

Sorrow that she had tried to still with the knife began to throb once more in her heart in tune with the words in the air. Her eyes closed slowly again, and her cold lips opened to silently mouth the words that had reopened the wound inside. Tears trickled out from beneath her eyelids, rolling over her face to fall upon the floor.

She was unable to catch her breath as the tears fell quicker, the agony in her wrists and in her chest now equal to each other, and she pulled her knees into her body, distorting the puddle of blood as they moved through it. Being in the foetal position did nothing to ease either pain, and she cried out to the empty room.

Her red and raw eyes lifted to the radio that had forced the world back upon her. Despair still gnawed at her heart but something was causing the tears to slow again, the ache in her chest easing a little.

Her traitorous eyes glided across from where the radio sat to the phone, sitting idly on its charger, just waiting to be picked up and put to use. Gingerly, she started to roll herself on to her knees, making sure that her bleeding arms stayed close to her chest. Excruciating pain shot from her arms through her whole body as one of her knees slipped in the red lake and her hands moved on their own to brace herself before she hit the floor face-first. Momentarily, her scream drowned out the radio.

Now that she had reached the decision to at least try and take back what she'd done she could feel each vital second speeding away from her. As carefully as she could, she raised herself again on to her knees, closing her eyes to fight off the wave of dizziness and light-headedness that rolled over her. All her body wanted to do now was sleep. She focused solely on the music as it neared its conclusion, struggling to stay conscious.

She gritted her teeth against the pain she knew would follow, and clambered to a standing position, head hanging down, obscured by her hair, the dizziness resuming its attack.

The song came to a stop, the DJ continued his chatter, and she stopped hearing it at all. Moving slowly and resolutely she headed to one of the drawers, pain renewed as she opened it to remove the tea towels. Only able to drape them across the cuts, she held her arms firmly pinned against her body as she crossed to the phone, wading through the room as if it was filled with water.

Ironically now fighting what she had sought so painfully to attain, she plucked the telephone from its place and dialled 999. Distantly, as black dots started an elegant and graceful dance before her eyes, she was aware of speaking to the operator, her voice slow and calm. She knew that she was answering the woman's questions accurately and lucidly, but the exact words spoken by either of them were lost to her behind the cloak of those multiplying dancing dots. The phone slipped from her grasp to clatter noisily upon the side, a streak of red across its white body. As those dots grew in number they seemed to be growing heavier and her head felt too weighted to hold up. She slumped to the floor, but it wasn't enough. Only by lying down did the weight in her head ease. She closed her eyes, knowing that she had changed her mind too late and that they were not going to reach her in time. And she realised that she didn't really mind, after all.

She fled from the light of the house, too preoccupied to notice the warm autumn breeze that lifted her hair from her face and caused her loose-fitting clothes to flutter about her body.

Clouds raced across the dark night sky above her, allowing only the briefest glimpses of the stars. The full moon also peered out sporadically, its beautiful light creating shadows that played upon the ground.

But she saw none of its beauty or mysticism. Her green eyes swam with tears, her face tracked with the trails of tears already shed. The air seemed to burn her eyes and she saw the faint light that shone through the clouds in prisms. Her legs moved her swiftly, yet she kept her arms still in front of her chest, crossed at the wrists yet not touching: it was a stance that she had become accustomed to.

Across the fields she ran, her trainers crunching over the short dry stalks of the recently cut grass, until she was no longer in sight of her home. Before she could slow down to stop, her foot caught on a hidden stone and she lost her balance. She fell heavily onto her knees and only by tensing her arm muscles at the last second was she able to prevent her hands from breaking her fall.

The furious sobs that she had so far been able to hold in broke free as she felt something cut through her jeans to attack her left leg. With her arms held to her chest, her head bowed and hidden by her hair, she rested on her knees and cried. Despair, grief, and loneliness swept through her; her heart ached with it all, and she was drowning in the autumn night.

Only when her chest ached from the strain, her sobs slowing and the flow of her tears drying, was she alerted to the sudden brightness of the night. She lifted her head and, through the parting in her hair, looked up at the moon.

The clouds that still moved swiftly in the sky seemed to change course so that not a single wisp blew across the full face of the moon.

As she gazed upwards she saw its beauty, yet felt only her despair grow. Without taking her eyes from the token of the Goddess that, although she still believed in, no longer offered the comfort it once had, she lifted her arms up. The sleeves of her white shirt fell to her elbows, exposing the bandages that were wrapped around her lower arms.

In the gesture of pleading, she felt a power building up in the air around her, felt a strength transferring itself from the moon above her and into her soul. The breeze began to build and blew her hair backwards, revealing all of her face, leaving her nothing to hide behind.

When she spoke, her voice was quiet, yet strong, and neither her gaze nor her tone faltered.

"I've always allowed fate to rule, believing that things will happen when they are meant to, trusting that everything will fall into place on their own. But I cannot wait any longer." Tears began to fall once more; still she forced herself on. "I'm lonely. In my body, in my mind, and in my heart. My soul aches with a longing that I can no longer deny."

She blinked back the tears and steadied herself, calling on all of her strength. "There has to be a reason I survived! There *has* to be!"

Her strength failed, flowed out of her, as a thick dark cloud passed across the moon, hiding its light once more. Slowly, carefully, she lowered her arms, again crossing them gently across her chest. Her head dropped as the torrent of tears began to escape her eyes.

In a whisper, she spoke one more word before her lament took her over. "Please."

The moon looked down on her, its light now unhindered and steady. It shared the girl's pain and mourned as she did. It mourned for what the girl had been through, the pain and loneliness that had so far been her life. But it mourned for more than that; it mourned for all that the girl would have to go through if her soul's mate was sent so soon. It mourned for the horrors and pain that she would have to endure.

Moved beyond words, the moon shone its light on the girl with the bandaged arms and, powerless to refuse her plea despite all of the reasons against, granted her request.

For a short time, the wind turned into a gale, almost pushing her backwards. And as the moon's blinding glow filled her vision she heard a whispering silver voice hidden within.

Listen for its call. Listen for the call of your spirit guide to lead your way. When the fire's descent enflames the clouds and burns the skies, when the ground falls from beneath your feet, and the wolf stares back into your eyes, give yourself over. Listen to its call to find the one who also seeks you. Follow the call and the passions of the wolf.

Her heart lifted and through the tears she smiled, feeling the despair that had engulfed her lighten. She pushed aside the sorrow that she had heard in that silent silver voice, and heard only the words.

Follow the call and the passions of the wolf.

Chapter One

"Can I help you?"

She looked at the kind-featured woman who looked back at her from the other side of the reception counter, the centre panel of safety glass that separated the reception from the waiting area presently pushed open. "I have an appointment at ten thirty to see Doctor Jackson."

"Do you have your appointment letter?"

She delved into her rucksack and brought out the folded letter. She opened it up and handed it to the woman behind the counter.

After a quick glance at the letter, she pushed a book through the gap. "Can you just sign in?"

Melissa dropped her bag by her feet and wrote her name in the book, noting as she jotted down the time that she was almost an hour early, before accepting her letter back.

"If you take a seat, Doctor Jackson will call you in."

"Thank you."

Luckily, the waiting area was unoccupied which meant that she had her choice of seats and she went directly to the chair in the corner. She looked briefly at the water cooler beside her as she sank into the soft cushions of the chair, but decided against having a drink – she didn't want to end up feeling like a child by having to ask her shrink if she could go to the toilet!

Smiling a little at the thought, she dropped her letter back into her navy-blue rucksack and took out the novel she had brought with her, using the bookmark as a lever to open it.

She soon lost herself in the world created by another person, looking up from the pages only when couple walked into the waiting area and sat opposite her. Exchanging a small shy smile, she dove back into the fictional landscape of scorching deserts and never-existing heroism.

"Melissa Adams?"

Melissa was catapulted out of the world that she held in her hands, her stomach turning nervously as she looked at the man who had called her name. Standing up, she put her book back into her bag and slung it across one shoulder. She then followed the man out of the waiting area through a keypad secured door that he held open for her.

"I'm sorry to have kept you waiting," he said as he led her through a white corridor. Glancing at her slightly bewildered expression, he laughed softly. "I guess you were too absorbed in your book to realise."

They were walking up a flight of stairs and Melissa felt uncomfortable in the sterile-white environment, but she managed a small laugh. "That's why I like reading: helps me forget where I am." She suddenly wished that she'd responded in a different way.

Instead of turning to analyse her as she'd expected in answer to her comment, he simply continued to smile. "Yeah, I'm the same. It's good to lose yourself in someone else's life for a while."

Her smile felt more natural as she followed him into a room on the left of the corridor. Although it was the same colour as the area she'd just walked through it didn't have the same clinical feel to it. The desk at the far side of the room, flanked by two large and full bookcases, was pushed back against the wall and there was no chair before it. The four low and comfortable looking chairs that sat in the middle of the light blue carpet were facing a low, round coffee table, a tan-coloured folder the only thing on it.

"Have a seat," he said, closing the door behind her as she walked in.

As she had in the waiting room she chose the chair the furthest from the door.

"Well," he said as he sat in the chair across from her. "As you've probably guessed, I'm Doctor Andrew Jackson."

She nodded, remaining quiet. She felt uneasy again, embarrassed at the prospect of having to talk to a total stranger about the personal aspects of her life.

"Do you know why you've been asked to come here?" He was sitting forwards on his chair, hands clasped and resting on his knees.

"I was referred to you by both my GP and the staff at the hospital." Her defences rose and she sat straighter in her chair, self-consciously pulling at the sleeves of her shirt so that the cuffs were at her knuckles; making sure that the bandages could not be seen.

He leant over and took hold of the folder before sitting back. He left it unopened on his lap. "Melissa, I need to make this clear to you."

As he looked at her through his circle-rimmed glasses she felt herself tense up. The idea of bolting out of the door started circling in her mind.

"I'm not here to try to trip you up or try to trick you."

Whatever she had been expecting him to say, it was not that. Melissa sagged a little in her chair.

"I'm not here to make you feel uncomfortable, or to make any judgements about anything you've done, or that you think." His eyes locked firmly onto hers. "I'm here to listen to you. I'm here to understand. And I'm here to help."

Careful not to let the folder slip from his lap, Andrew leant forwards, noticing a mist that had started to form in her eyes. "Anything and everything you say to me will always be confidential; legally, I'm not allowed to disclose anything that we speak about. And although I will be writing in this –" he patted the folder – "it's never left lying around anywhere."

All Melissa could do was nod – she had no idea of how to respond to his efforts to make her feel more comfortable.

"You were referred to me because you tried – and very nearly succeeded – to kill yourself. Everybody is very worried about you, and we want to make sure that you don't feel like you need to resort to that again. You're not on your own; I'm here to try to help you through whatever you're struggling with. But in order for me to be able to help you, Melissa, you need to be able to be honest with me in everything. Okay?"

Melissa smiled and tears tracked quickly down her cheeks. She wiped them away with her thumbs, her fingers holding the cuffs of her sleeves to prevent them from sliding up, and nodded. "Okay," she whispered.

"Okay." He opened the folder and took a pen from its clip on the inside of the cover. "Now, this first meeting is basically for us to get to know each other a little, for me to get some basic details. If there's something specific you want to mention, at any time, just go for it; even if it has no connection to what we've been talking about."

Her mouth felt dry and she wished that she'd had a drink while waiting. Her nerves started to grow again and she increased her grip on her shirt cuffs.

"So," he said as he sat back and relaxed in the chair, still holding the folder. "Is there anything specific that you wanted to talk about, Melissa?"

Melissa could feel her hands sweating, could feel her heart speeding up. There was an invisible spotlight before her that had been switched on, and the unseen light made it too clear for her to be seen. She focussed on the man in front of her, saw the gentle brown eyes looking back at her, and the spotlight disappeared and she could breathe easy again.

"I don't know." She hated how weak she sounded, and rearranged herself a little, laughing self-consciously. "I don't know what I'm supposed to say. What am I supposed to talk about?"

"As I said, anything you want. What's the dominant thing you're thinking, right now?"

She chuckled quietly. "Aside from how uncomfortable I'm

feeling?" She continued to smile as he smiled at her. "Well, I guess the obvious thing is this." She raised her sleeve-encased arms.

"Do you want to talk about that, Melissa?"

"I don't know." She could feel her cheeks heating up and dropped her eyes, wishing that she'd worn her hair down instead of up, wishing that she had something to hide behind. A lump formed in her throat and her eyes began to sting. "I guess I think I might need to."

Melissa looked away from her arms, where she imagined she could see the bandages below the baggy sleeves, to try to find something else to focus on. Looking at the bookcase on the left she trained her sight on a large green book, concentrating so that she could see every bump on its spine.

Smiling, she looked back at the man who waited patiently, knowingly, for her to compose herself. "I don't know how to start."

Andrew looked down at the file on his lap. "You were unconscious when they found you?"

She nodded. "Yeah."

"Did they tell you anything about it?"

"Yeah, one of the doctors talked me through it when he was asking me all the questions."

"And what did he tell you?"

She sat herself straight and looked at him determinedly. She was *not* going to cry! "He told me that the police had arrived first and broken down the door. The paramedics got there about five minutes later."

"Why were the police there?"

"Apparently I'd told the operator that the door was locked."

"Apparently?"

"Yeah." Melissa smiled a hard smile. "I don't really remember that too well. I mean, I remember talking on the phone, but not what I said."

Andrew nodded for her to continue.

"Anyway, the cops had tried to put pressure on my arms to try to stop the bleeding, and then the paramedics turned up and took me to the hospital. I was stitched up, given five units of blood, and they started my heart again when it stopped."

"Your heart stopped?"

"Yes."

"So you *did* die?"

"Yes."

"How did you feel when you woke up in the hospital?"

"Disorientated. Surreal, like I'd wandered into a Salvador Dali painting."

"You know Salvador Dali's work?"

She nodded, smiling at how shocked he seemed by that. "I love his work. It's incredible."

"My favourite's *Swans Reflecting Elephants*." Andrew said, watching as she grinned widely, her eyes sparkling.

"I love that one! But my favourites are *The Metamorphosis of Narcissus* and *Solitude*."

He leant forwards a little, her obvious knowledge of the artist's paintings capturing his attention. "I remember the first one, but can't picture *Solitude*."

A little of the happiness faded from her eyes to be replaced by a gentle sorrow. "It's quite an empty painting. There's a figure leaning in towards a rock, I think it's a woman, and it looks as if she's merging with it; there are shells and rocks forming on one shoulder. And that's all that's really in it."

He sat back again, regarding her with interest. "Why do you like those paintings?"

"I like all of his work; just how nothing is ever what it first appears to be, that you have to *search* for what's actually there."

"But why those two in particular?"

Melissa knew that the answer would reveal a little too much about her, but strangely it now seemed unimportant. For someone who had spent her life not trusting anyone, she trusted this man completely. "*Metamorphosis* because I think it's about self-perception. The rocks that mirror each other in the foreground aren't true reflections of the other – one is positive and the other negative; and neither is the truth because we all have positive and negative aspects that make us whole."

"And *Solitude*?"

"Because it's a painting filled with loneliness. And that's something I understand."

It was Andrew who broke the silence when it started to develop an uneasy quality. "So why did waking up in the hospital leave you feeling like that?"

"I don't know. Just that everything seemed far away from me; even if I tried to touch things that were next to me, I would feel miles away from them. That how close they appeared was only an illusion, just a trick of the mind." She laughed a little, shaking her head. "It doesn't make much sense."

"Were things like that before? Was that how things appeared?"

"No. Then it was all smoke and fire." Embarrassed and shocked at herself, she met his eyes briefly – but it was long enough to see the uncertainty there.

"Smoke and fire?"

Melissa nodded, tears threatening again. She wanted to expand on what she'd said but felt incapable of speech.

"In what way was it like smoke and fire, Melissa?"

She fought inside herself, struggling to form some kind of answer to his question. As she was beginning to believe that no answer was going to come, she had a sudden flash of memory. She could see the knife that she was holding at her wrist, could see the way that the skin dimpled gently before rising again as the point slipped through. She could see the small and soft spot of blood as it bloomed tenderly where the metal entered her arm. Then she heard a whisper of the song that she was growing to think of as hers.

Hold on, hold on.

"Melissa?"

She realised that she was smiling to herself while lost in her reverie, and laughed as she brought herself back. "Sorry. Kind of wandered then."

"That's okay."

Looking at him, she suspected that he wasn't aware of the concern that showed on his face, but wasn't going to draw attention to it. "I was just thinking how to explain.

"My whole life has felt like it was made entirely out of smoke and fire. Things have either had no substance, nothing to grasp or hold onto, like smoke. Or they have engulfed me, burned me so badly that I didn't *want* to hold onto them, like fire. There was never anything that was solid."

"Was it the smoke or the fire that made you want to kill yourself?"

"The fire. I could cope with not feeling – it was like living in a dream, where I noticed everything, but nothing was real. It was when things felt real that—"

A phone started to ring, cutting her off.

"Shit!" Andrew stood and walked to the desk against the wall, fumbling open a bag. "I'm really sorry about this, Melissa. I was sure I'd turned it off." He brought the small silver phone out just as it stopped ringing. He turned it off and dropped it back in.

"Sorry," he said again as he sat back down.

"That's okay." But she had lost what she was about to say, her self-consciousness had been summoned back by the phone's noise and she felt uncertainty start to creep back in.

Andrew also knew that the moment had gone and that it would be destructive to try to recapture it. "So, you like Salvador Dali. Any other artists?"

Melissa shook her head. "He's the only one who's ever really stood out to me and caught my attention."

"Do you sketch or paint?"

Laughing, she began to relax again. "No, I can't draw." She hesitated, then added, "I do write poems though."

"Yeah?"

She nodded, feeling colour flood into her face.

"What type of poetry?"

She shrugged, embarrassed that she had mentioned her hobby at all. "Just poems. They're not any good, but I enjoy writing them."

"Oh, I'm sure they are." Andrew was used to seeing self-doubt and low self-confidence in his patients and, although it was a shame to see it in the girl opposite him, it came as no great surprise. "How long have you been writing them?"

"Since I was a kid."

"Have you ever tried to have them published?"

Melissa nodded. "Yeah, when I was younger. I haven't really looked into it since – I think the last time I submitted any of them to a publisher I was about fifteen."

"Maybe it's something you should think about again."

"Maybe." She said this without any real conviction. Although she knew that her poems weren't bad, could actually be considered by some to be good, there was just no way any of them were up to publishing standard; and there was no way that she was going to put herself through the rejection.

Andrew looked at the clock that was above the desk. "Well, we're getting close to the end of our first session, Melissa."

It was difficult for her to understand why, but the prospect of the appointment being over so soon actually made her a little unhappy.

"But, I wanted to ask you one last thing."

"Okay."

"What do you want to get out of our sessions?"

Melissa could only look blankly at him. "What do you mean?"

Andrew closed the folder and leant forwards to drop it back onto the table. "How do you think it'll help, talking to me? What do you hope will happen as a result of our meetings?"

She felt stupid and naive. "I don't know."

"Well, I want you to think about it before our next appointment. Okay?"

She nodded, hating how unsure she now felt as a result of that question, watching as Andrew went again to his bag.

With his large black leather-bound diary, he sat back down. "And speaking of our next appointment…" Using his finger, he scrolled down the pages. "Next Wednesday? About ten thirty?" He looked at her expectantly.

"Yeah, that sounds okay." She watched as he wrote her name on the line, and she accepted the small card on which he jotted the appointment time.

They both stood and, after retrieving her bag from the floor beside her, she followed him out of the room as they retraced their steps.

"So was it as bad as you thought it would be?" Andrew asked with a grin as they descended the stairs.

She laughed lightly. "No, nowhere near as bad."

Back in the waiting room, just on the other side of the keypad-locked door, she turned to face him.

In the two weeks since her suicide attempt Melissa had kept her arms covered and in front of her; she had avoided doing anything that could possible expose or put pressure on the injuries that she had inflicted. And yet she now found herself extending her right arm out.

"Thank you, Doctor Jackson."

He was pleasantly surprised by the gesture and took the offered hand, being sure to shake it as gently as possible, mindful of the wounds. "Andrew."

Smiling gently, she folded her hand back in front of her. "Thank you, Andrew."

"I'll see you next week, Melissa. And remember to give some thought to what I asked."

"I will."

He turned and went back through the door and Melissa turned to leave. She changed course though and walked to the water cooler – her throat was so dry and she desperately needed a drink. The cold water felt so good as it went down her throat and she drank two cups in a row. She put the cup in the bin and once more turned to sign out so that she could leave.

She didn't stop moving, her feet continued to carry her towards the desk, but time seemed to have slowed down and stretched.

Behind the lenses of the oval-rimmed glasses, those warm soft-hazel eyes looked back at her and for a moment Melissa saw nothing else. His tawny hair trailed slightly past his ears; it was mostly straight but the strands that should have fallen over his eyes had a natural kink to them, sweeping them away.

As they passed each other, the man heading to the chairs, the smile that he sent her way made the world fade in comparison.

She wanted to turn around, to take a seat next to him and simply talk to him, even if it meant just finding out his name. Yet she had reached the counter and was already picking up the pen. Quickly she wrote the time down next to her name but paused before dropping the pen.

The last name in the book, two lines down from her own caught her for a moment and she smiled: Marshall Bell.

She pushed the book back through and began to walk out of the door. Passing through, she glanced to her right to see Marshall looking at her. Smiling, and feeling like a schoolgirl with a crush, she walked out into the hot autumn sunshine.

She threw her bag and keys gently onto the table in the corner and collapsed onto the sofa, letting the silence of the house infect her and drive out all residue of the outside world. Her thoughts were shocked into stillness by the tranquillity and Melissa revelled in it. When they started to clamour through the quiet, she sighed and reached over to the answer phone.

"Message received nineteenth of September at one eighteen pm." The robotic-sounding voice was followed by a brief high-pitched beep.

There was a short silence before a woman's voice spoke out of the machine. "Melissa? It's me. I was just...erm, I was just checking to see how the...er...the appointment went. Ring whe—"

The positive feelings that had followed after speaking to Andrew disappeared in a second at the sound of her mother's voice and Melissa cut the voice off as she hit the button harshly, too keen to stop her mother's words to care about damaging the machine. Or hurting herself.

She winced at the slight twinge that she felt beneath the bandage. Her eyes closed and she could feel her face forming the unattractive set that always came upon her when she thought about the woman who had given her life twenty-three years before.

Striving to purge herself of the anger that had started to take a hold, Melissa turned her attention to the question that Andrew had asked at the end of the session, forcing her mind to stay fixed on that alone.

Chapter Two

"Do you still need to wear the bandages?"

Melissa looked away from the window opposite, away from the lines that the rain was forming on the glass, to look at Andrew. "No. The cuts are healing really well. I got the stitches out a couple of days ago."

"Why do you still wear them?"

She blushed and looked down at her arms, seeing that the sleeves had risen a little exposing the smallest hint of the white material. Briskly, she pulled the sleeves back down. "I'm just not comfortable *not* wearing them while I'm out." Looking at Andrew, almost daring him to mock her, she added, "I just don't want anyone staring at the cuts. I don't want anyone feeling sorry for me. I don't like pity."

There was an edge to her today that hadn't been present at their first session, and Andrew suspected that her reluctance to talk wasn't due to any unease or nerves as it had the week before; something had happened to put that hard glint in her eyes.

He regarded her silently for a minute, watching as she turned her gaze back to the window. Her light brown hair was again in a high ponytail, giving her the outward appearance of someone a little younger. But her green eyes shone with a strength that could only be grown by more years than she had experienced – or by intensely painful ordeals.

"Melissa?" He waited until she was looking at him again before continuing. "Did you think about what I asked you last week?"

The glint disappeared from her, her eyes softening. "Yeah, I did."

"Good. So, tell me, Melissa, what do you want to achieve as a result of our sessions?"

She smiled gently, feeling herself becoming totally disarmed.

"Do you want the long answer or the short one?"

Grinning, he replied, "Both."

"Okay. Long answer first. I want to work through everything that's happened to me; I want to move on from my past and be able to start *thinking* about having some sort of future; I want to be happy living my life."

Andrew nodded. "And the short answer?"

Sadly, she smiled again. There was no longer any trace of the hard strength that she had carried with her for the last few days. All that was left was a lost girl. "I want to find myself again."

Andrew had jotted everything down in her file and now looked at her again. "You feel like you've lost yourself?"

Melissa had her eyes closed, and tears escaped as she nodded. With an effort, she wiped the tears away and opened her eyes. She couldn't look at Andrew though, so she picked a spot on the table and stared at that. "I lost who I was a very long time ago." She tried to force a smile but didn't quite manage it.

Andrew looked at her, uncertain about the best way to proceed. Her sudden change from hard strength to utter sadness left his usual methods of approaching a person's past, redundant. He glimpsed the thin silver chain that was around her neck, but was unable to see what the chain held as it snaked beneath her shirt.

"Are you religious, Melissa?"

She lifted her eyes, and there was nothing bitter in the strength that had reappeared; it was full of pride. "Yes."

"What religion are you?"

She hooked a finger beneath her chain and slid the pendant out to show him. The small pentagram was encircled by a thin band, and a small hematite stone sat in its centre. She let it drop onto the outside of her shirt.

"I'm not totally sure what that represents," Andrew said, etching the symbol into his mind.

That glint appeared in her eyes once more, again daring him

to ridicule her in some way. "I'm a pagan."

He decided to tackle the obvious issue head-on. "Are you expecting me to make fun of you?"

Melissa's eyes did soften slightly but caution was still clear as she looked at Andrew. "Most people do."

"Well, I won't. I don't know much about paganism but I *do* know that it shows a reverence for life and nature. And I can only feel respect for those who respect others."

Feeling a little ashamed of her defensiveness, Melissa nodded. "Sorry, I'm just a bit on edge. And when I'm like this the barriers go up a little higher than normal."

"That's okay. But you need to keep in mind what I told you last week, Melissa. I'm not here to pass any kind of judgement. I'm just here to help."

"I know."

"So, what is it that's put you on edge?"

It was difficult for her not to allow the anger to boil to the surface nor allow her features to form those hardened lines that she despised so much; but she managed it to some degree, although she was very aware of the amount that did show through her eyes. "A couple of things."

A part of her wished that he'd drop it, would just leave it alone, but another part of her hoped that he would push for an answer. Andrew did neither; he just sat and waited for her to add more. He continued to sit there, patiently looking at her. Eventually, Melissa admitted defeat and broke the silence.

"When I had my stitches taken out, the nurse who did it…"

"What about the nurse, Melissa?"

"The way she looked at me…" She gulped past the lump that had formed in her throat, summoning the anger to deter the sadness. "I told you earlier: I *don't like* people feeling sorry for me."

"And she did?"

"It was just the way she was looking at me, like I was the most pitiful person ever! And she was talking to me as if I were a child; you know, really softly, the way you'd speak to a kid. And after she'd finished, when she told me I could go, she patted my arm – I was half-expecting her to give me a lolly or a sticker for being so well behaved!" Melissa was aware that her voice had grown higher and louder and that she had become more agitated. Her hands had rolled into fists, her fingernails digging gently into the palms of her hands. She forced them to relax, and looked at Andrew squarely. "I just don't like pity."

Andrew sat quietly for a moment, then uttered one word. "Why?"

"Why what?"

"What is it about people feeling sorry for you that you don't like?"

She searched his eyes. "I just don't like it."

"But *why*? What is it about someone showing you sympathy that makes you so annoyed?"

Whether the tears that slipped from her eyes were from sadness or anger Melissa didn't know, didn't care. "It makes me feel weak," she whispered.

"Weak?"

"I can do things for myself. I don't need anyone else for *anything*. I can cope on my own; I'm strong enough to do things without help. But when someone looks at me like that I feel like I can't cope, that it means I *do* need help, and I don't!" Roughly she wiped her tears away. "I refuse to depend on anyone."

"When someone feels sympathy for you it makes you feel that maybe you're *not* strong enough to cope?"

"Yes."

Andrew dropped her folder to the floor beside his chair and leant forwards. "Letting people help you doesn't make you weak, Melissa. Depending on someone to help you through the good *and* the bad things that happen doesn't mean you can't cope."

"But if you depend on someone, rely on another person, it just hurts more when they let you down."

He leant back again, pushing his glasses a little further up his nose. "If you let someone help it'll make it easier for them to hurt you. So you don't allow yourself to *feel* like you need help. Have I got that right?"

She nodded, hating him for making it seem so stupid. She fixed her eyes back onto the windowpane, tracing the small rivers as they ran down the glass. She was aware of her cheeks burning and of the cool lines that tracked down her face.

"Melissa? Melissa, look at me."

Barriers as high as she could get them in her green eyes, she turned back to him.

"Why did you try and kill yourself?"

It was blunt and straight to the point, and it created the same effect as being slapped. She opened her mouth to speak but closed it when she had nothing to say.

It was what he had hoped for. Asking her that question, direct and without any sense of discretion, had wiped out her barriers and, for the time being, had chased away her anger. Andrew knew that she wasn't ready to answer that question and he was not going to push for one; but the fact that he'd asked it at all had shocked her to where she needed to be for them to be able to move forwards.

She was pulling at the sleeves of her shirt, struggling to try to find a response, *any* response.

"It's okay, Melissa. You don't have to answer that." Andrew did feel guilty at the magnitude of relief that filled her eyes as she looked at him. "You said there were a couple of things that had put you on edge. One was the nurse's attitude towards you. What else?"

At the thought of the second trigger she should have felt angry, but Melissa was so relieved that he had moved swiftly on from the most difficult question that the anger stayed away. "My mum."

"What about her, Melissa?"

She laughed briefly, harshly. "Everything."

As she looked away, back at the rain-decorated window, Andrew picked up her file again. Silently, he waited for her to continue.

Thinking about how to start as she watched the rain was a bad idea. How she had felt for the last few days, the fury and hatred that caused her to feel so unattractive, pushed away the temporary calmness that Andrew had forced on her. Her eyes closed and she trained her focus on her breathing, the techniques that she used for meditation helping to restrain the worst of it. A little, anyway.

"She's everything I hate about people."

"In what way?"

His voice seemed dull in the red-coloured darkness behind her eyes, and it was too much. It was too similar to how things had seemed as she lay bleeding on the kitchen floor. Hastily she opened her eyes.

"In *every* way. She's so bigoted – about *every*thing! She's racist, she's homophobic, she looks down her nose at everyone. She thinks that she suffers more than anyone else, but that she's better at everything! And the world *has* to revolve around her – and if it doesn't then she tries to make it!"

She offered him a strained smile. "I *do* realise what I'm like when I talk about my mum. I try not to let her views get to me, but it's not easy."

"Do you love her?"

"I've thought about how I feel about her a lot. And I *do* love her – she's my mother. But I don't *like* her, as a person. I don't like who she's become, who I've realised she is. I don't have any respect for her. I don't trust her, and I tend not to believe most of what she says. There's just too much that I can't forgive her for."

"Like what, Melissa?"

She searched his eyes and although she found only a genuine interest in her well-being, it wasn't enough for her yet. "I can't get into that stuff yet. It's too soon."

He didn't try and pursue it any further. "When was the last time you spoke to her, Melissa?"

"A few days after I cut my wrists. The hospital refused to let me out unless I had a 'support network'. I asked her to leave an hour after I got home, and I've avoided speaking to her since. She has rung me a couple of times, but I only returned the call once – and only when I knew she'd be out; I left a message on her answer phone."

"When did she last ring?"

"Last week. She asked how things had gone with you."

"Did you ring her back? Or was it before that call that you rang her?"

"Before."

"You really can't stand even speaking to her?"

"No."

"Melissa, are you okay still talking about her?"

She looked down at her hands and saw that they had closed into fists of their own volition. The nails dug deep into her palms and she forced herself to loosen her grip. Determinedly she concentrated on relaxing every part of her body. Only when she was sure that she had relinquished her anger did she answer Andrew. "No. I think talking about my mother, in any respect, will have to wait."

"That's okay. I did, actually, want to ask you about something you said last week."

"What?"

"'Smoke and fire'." It was a little unsettling how quick the barriers appeared. "It was really poetic sounding. I was just wandering where that phase came from."

"It's from a two-part poem that I wrote a couple of years ago."

"Yeah?"

"Yeah."

"Do you think I could read it?"

Melissa's first response, her gut reaction, was to laugh and say 'no, never'. But the idea that he was interested in reading something personal of hers didn't seem completely scary. The idea made her nervous, but she was curious if he would say anything positive about them. And that made her decide.

"I think I'd like you to."

Both feeling pleased, the session moved on with the two of them at ease, yet neither of them wanting to spoil the comfortable feeling by discussing anything too intense.

There were two deep cardboard boxes stacked one on top of the other in the back of her wardrobe. The one on the top had writing printed in thick black pen. The one below wasn't marked in any way. As Melissa moved the clothes that hung in front of them out of the way and picked up the topmost box she glanced briefly at the other. Before the pang of combined anger and despair could transform into something worse, she closed the wardrobe door, shutting the remaining box back into darkness.

She knelt on the floor with the box in front of her. Grinning at the thin film of dust that coated the lid she blew across the top, playing a thousand scenes from a thousand corny films in her head as she did. She was a little disappointed that only a little dust rose into the air and not the full storm that she had pictured in her mind.

Looking through some of the loose pages caused a pain in her heart that she hadn't anticipated. Each poem she glanced at reignited the pain that had inspired her to write them. Three poems down Melissa simply started to scan the titles in a vain attempt at keeping away her past.

With the two pages that held the words that she had been looking for in her hand she sat back with her legs stretched out before her and read what she had written so long ago.

Smoke...
I reach out to touch you
And my hand moves through the air.
I try to touch your lips
But you're no longer there.
Your image is illusion,
Your face fades from sight,
Your warm breath upon my neck
Is only the breeze of night.
Air has more substance,
It's easier to hold,
Than the non-existent figure
Of a past that is now cold.
Each and every thing I see
Seems a million miles away;
Each thing I try to touch
Is always kept at bay.
What is the point of anything
When nothing is close to real?
When everything has faded
And there's nothing left to feel?
When the good, with the bad,
Is viewed through a screen
Of emptiness and numbness,
When nothing's really seen?
There has to be a reason
For my presence in this world;
I'm waiting to find the answer,
The flower to be unfurled.
But it doesn't matter how
Hard I try to find;
The answer's always lost to me,
No truth of any kind
Is presented to my aching soul;

My empty and hollow heart
Waits for something to fill it,
For anything to start.
But smoke is the essence of my life,
Is every part of me,
And when I look in the mirror
The smoke is all I see.

...And Fire
Savagely it attacks and
Burns within my soul.
It ravages my thoughts and dreams
And eats up every goal.
Its blaze flickers in my eyes,
The anger, grief and pain;
It floods through my aching shape,
It surges through my veins.
Consuming my hopes of a future
That can never be,
The past attacks my present
And will never let me see
Anything of any good
That I know must be around;
Love and joy shrouded
And with chains completely bound.
And as the flames of pain
Sink deeper in my heart
I feel the call of my blood,
The paint of my pain-fuelled art.
'Cause when that knife drives deeper,
When my flesh allows it in,
Those flames dampen slightly
And I feel that I could win.
With blood flowing over

My skin in vine-like streaks
The temporary serenity
Soon climbs to its peak.
Then the dwindling flames of the fire
That had never really died
Flares up, that well-known torment
That refuses to let me hide.
The agony of scorching heat
Is never gone for long,
No matter how much I use the knife
To let the blood sing its song.
I look into the mirror
To see the fire caged inside,
The pain held trapped in my blood
Until the knife sets free the tide.

Unsure at how she should be reacting to the poems, she walked down to the kitchen with the papers in hand, longing for a very strong cup of coffee. She was filling the kettle up when the phone began to ring.

After the third ring the answer phone kicked in, prompting the caller to leave a message, which Melissa's mother began to do in a slurred voice.

"Hi, Sweetheart, it's Mum. Guess you didn't get my message last week—"

A loud sound of cracking replaced the woman's drunken speech as Melissa ripped the cable from the wall. Tears filled her venomous eyes as she dropped the cable from her fingers and walked back into the kitchen, ensuring that her eyes didn't stray to the knife set on the side; she didn't think she'd be able to fight the compulsion if they did.

Chapter Three

Each line he added, each small scratch upon her skin, sent ripples of delicious pain through her. It was such a strange sensation, and as enjoyable as it had been the first time he had touched her with the needle almost four weeks ago. The pain didn't go as deep into her flesh as the pain she had caused herself in the past, but it felt more intense. Knowing that she was changing herself forever, that the stinging was there for a positive reason and not a negative one, made the experience sweeter than she could have imagined.

She lay face down on the reclining black chair, only her bra on the upper part of her body. Her head rested on her arms and she looked sideways at the photos and designs that littered the walls within her view. Some of them were very basic, mere outlines of pictures; others were so detailed and incredibly, skilfully composed that Melissa had trouble accepting that they had been produced on skin rather than on canvas.

On the other side of her, Paul sat on a stool, leaning forwards with his left hand gently placed on the small of her naked back while the right expertly scored patterns in black, occasionally stopping to wipe away blood when it obscured the blue picture he traced. The sound of the needle, a thrumming that was slightly reminiscent of a dentist's drill, was stopped and he placed it on the moveable table next to him, making sure the wires weren't hanging where they could be caught. He wiped her back with an antiseptic wipe, studying the artwork intently to make sure that he hadn't missed any part of it out. Satisfied Paul started to remove his black latex gloves.

"All done, Melissa."

She raised her head from her arms. "Already?"

"Yeah. Come and have a look – see what you think."

Not feeling the least big shy, Melissa walked over to the far side of the room and looked into the tall mirror, waiting for Paul to fetch the smaller hand mirror. He angled it slightly to the left and Melissa grinned as the reflection of her back was bounced into view. It was difficult for her to believe that she was seeing herself.

"As good as you thought it would be?"

"Loads better!" She had a hunch that she wouldn't be able to stop smiling for a long time.

After Paul cleaned her back again and covered the new addition to her large tattoo with thin dressings to prevent blood transferring onto her clothes, Melissa slipped back into her shirt.

Back in the front of the shop, surrounded by hundreds and hundreds of designs pinned onto the walls, Melissa handed Paul four twenty-pound notes.

Confused, he tried to hand one of them back. "You only owe me sixty pounds; you've already paid two tens."

"I think you undercharged me though," she replied, still grinning.

Paul opened his mouth to argue but was cut off when the bell over the shop door rang. "Hi, Michael."

Melissa's stomach rolled pleasurably as the shop's new caller met her eyes. She could feel her cheeks reddening as he walked closer to where she and Paul stood.

"Hi, Paul." He broke his eyes away from her briefly to greet the tattooist before turning back to her. "Hi."

"Hi." She longed to say something clever, interesting, intriguing. But those sexy dark blue eyes on her had stolen all of her thoughts – well, not *all*. But the thought she *did* have only made her more flustered.

"Were you wanting to book in for your next one, Michael?"

When he looked away from her once more Melissa saw the knowing look on Paul's face, the meaningful smile he gave her. She stood silent as they discussed appointment times, and found herself appraising the lines of his body underneath the jeans and shirt. She could see how toned he was, the contours of the muscles in his arms. Melissa just had time to raise her eyes as he turned back in her direction; but out of the corner of her eye she noticed Paul's widening grin. *He* had seen.

Catching her eyes once again Michael said goodbye to her and walked out of the shop. Before continuing on his way he turned his head to look at her again, smiled, and disappeared from view.

Melissa was aware of promising to show Paul the tattoo when it had healed completely, of promising to visit when she wanted another tattoo, of then leaving the shop to go home. But hidden behind her automatic responses she was lost in a daydream of the man she had met fleetingly; lost in a world where she ran his fingers through his dark brown hair and ran her hands over the figure beneath the clothes.

When she got home she walked directly to the bathroom and took off her shirt. Straining, she peeled off the dressings and gently washed her back. After patting it dry she rubbed antiseptic cream onto the tattoo, letting the feel of the raised skin guide her hands.

She thought of putting her shirt back on then smiled. There was no actual need for her to wear it, she wasn't going to be going out or anything, She walked through the living room towards the kitchen, pressing the button on her answer phone as she passed without any sense of unease. When the robotic voice announced that she had no messages her smile widened.

There had been no messages for the last two weeks, no phone calls at all, and because of that silence Melissa had felt happier. She was glad that she had taken both pieces of Andrew's advice.

"So? Is it finished?"

They were sitting in their accustomed chairs in the room, both relaxed and comfortable in each other's company.

"Yeah, Paul finished it on Friday. I've just got to wait for it to heal properly and it'll be done."

"How does it look?"

The smile on her face was complete and illuminated her eyes, making them sparkle. "Brilliant! I mean, it'll look better in about a week, but it's good!"

Her smile was infectious. "Glad you did it?"

"Definitely!"

"I have to admit, though, it wasn't what I expected you to do." He laughed a little at her questioning gaze. "I'm not sure what I expected you to do when I suggested you do something you've always wanted to do, but getting a tattoo wasn't it!"

There was no defensiveness in her, hadn't been for their last three meetings; she just felt too happy to feel as though she needed to shield herself from anything.

"I love tattoos, always have. I've just never had the courage to get any done."

"Until now."

"Yeah, until now."

They sat in a companionable silence for a moment. "Still no phone calls?"

"Nope! Another good suggestion from you, Andrew." She laughed softly. "I don't know why I didn't think about changing my phone number before. But I'm glad I've finally done it. Just knowing that her voice isn't going to greet me when I check my messages…" She shook her head. "You just can't understand how good that feels!"

"No, I can't. But I'm glad it's helped." Andrew nodded at the small black book in Melissa's hand. "So, what's that?"

"A side effect of having my tattoo done." She couldn't help but smile at the confusion on his face. "I figured that if I was brave enough to have my tattoo done then I was brave enough for this." Without adding more, she walked over to him and placed the book in his hands before sitting back in her chair. "I put the ribbon where you need to open it."

He used the ribbon to open the pages and looked down at the large elegant writing. As he saw the word that appeared on the top of the page, he glanced swiftly at her. "Your poems?"

She nodded. "I found that book at a bookshop, and just thought it would be perfect; I kind of wanted all my poems in one place – easy to find. And add to."

"'Smoke…'" he said, almost in a whisper, before falling into silence to read the two part poem that he had been so curious about.

To begin with Melissa sat and watched him, looking at his eyes as they scanned across the words, looking to catch any sign of reaction from him. But as her nervousness started to grow she turned to look out of the window.

"Melissa?"

She looked back at him, slightly anxious as she noted that the book was closed and the intensity of his gaze as he locked his eyes with hers.

"They're brilliant."

Embarrassed, but in a good way, she shook her head. "They're okay; but they're not *that* good."

"They're brilliant." Andrew simply stated again. "They're fantastically written. The language you use is so expressive. And they flow so well – there's no abruptness to them."

It was purely a habitual reaction as she searched his words for hidden insincerities or veiled mockery; most of her felt pleased by his words, yet Melissa had to fight hard not to argue with what he'd said and to just accept it. "Thank you."

"You're welcome. Thank you for letting me read them." He handed her back the book. "You mentioned adding to them?"

"Yeah, I've got a couple more ideas that I'm messing around with."

"Like the two I've read?"

"Not exactly." She could feel her cheeks reddening. "Not as depressing, and more…"

"Adult?" Andrew finished as she struggled for the words.

Her cheeks flushed deeper but she laughed. "Yeah, more adult. Not explicit exactly, but…suggestive."

"Completely different subject matter, then."

Continuing to blush, Melissa just smiled, her mind flashing back to the man she had met briefly in the tattooists, as it always seemed to the past few days.

She eased herself into the bath, the hot water moving up her body as she lay down, the bubbles moving around her. An incense stick burned softly on the far side of the bathroom, its gentle scent filling the room. Melissa sank deeper in the water, allowing her shoulders to feel the benefit of the heat. The black clip on the top of her head held her hair up and out of the bubbles' reach, only a few rogue strands having escaped.

She closed her eyes and let herself sink into everything around her; the temperature of the bath was making her sweat; the sweetness of the rose-scented incense circled around her; and the stillness, the quietness of the world she was in. She savoured every sensation, allowing no thoughts to pollute or interrupt the contentment that filled her.

The water started to cool, the incense finished burning, and Melissa opened her eyes. As she had lain there the sensitive skin that had recently been parted by a knife had started to throb a little, not totally unpleasantly, in the heat. After lifting her arms clear of the water, bubbles slipping from her skin, she looked at the scars.

She ran her right index finger over the scar on her left arm, feeling the way the skin dipped slightly. She felt so distant from the person she had been only forty-two days ago. The memory of that time, although it felt fresh and raw at some moments, presently had faded, as if it had taken place years ago instead of merely weeks. Although nothing momentous had happened to her since she had tried to kill herself she was happy simply because of the calmness of her existence; and due to the pain of what she considered her past-life, that feeling was alien to her. As was the fact that the almost-invisible impact upon her life had come about simply by having someone to talk to, someone just to listen.

While adrift in the cooling, but still warm, bubble bath Melissa thought of what had happened in that short space of time; the new muteness of her mother; sharing her poems, and writing again; and her tattoo! Something that she had always wanted to do, but had only found the courage after speaking to Andrew. And most importantly, she had begun to think about how her life *could* become, how *good* it could be if she let it. If she held on to the courage that she had evoked to get her tattoo.

Andrew had advised her against thinking about working again too soon, of trying to push herself to run when she was just starting to learn to walk again. And she intended to take his advice on that as well – but she had started *thinking* about thinking of returning to work. And the idea of having something resembling a normal life, of earning again and returning to independence, filled her with pride.

A towel wrapped around her body and her hair, still dry apart from those few errant strands, cascading softly over her bare shoulders she settled upon the sofa with her legs tucked up beside her, a hot cup of coffee held between two hands. Instead of the main light, Melissa sat in the soft glow of her tall lamp.

When the cup was half-empty she put it on the table beside her and picked up her black mobile phone. Astonished, she could only stare at the screen as she slid it open, as the words '1 missed call' and '1 new voicemail' shone out at her.

Her stomach churned uncomfortably, the fleeting thought of the possibility of her mum having phoned flitted through her mind before she dismissed it as impossible – she had never given the woman her mobile number.

She pressed the button that connected her to her voicemail

and, hands shaking slightly, Melissa held the phone to her ear. In a voice that lost nothing by being heard over a phone, she heard her own name being spoken. Goosebumps broke out all over her body, the hair on the back of her neck stood on end, purely by the sound of that voice.

"Melissa, it's Michael Ellis – we met at the tattooist's on Friday. Hope you don't mind, but I nagged Paul for your name and number. I just wondered if you fancied catching a film, or maybe going for a drink sometime. I'll give you a call again tomorrow and ask you properly."

Melissa saved the message when prompted, and immediately listened to it again. After the third time hearing it she cut off the call and just sat, seeing nothing in front of her, just feeling the butterflies dancing in her stomach as, in her head, she heard that message repeated over and over.

Chapter Four

Anaesthetic couldn't have numbed her any more than she already felt as she walked to the door. The smoke and fire of her past seemed to have joined somehow – everything felt distant yet simultaneously blindingly brilliant.

Facing the door, Melissa felt his presence behind her, could smell the tantalising scent of his aftershave enveloping her like a cloud. Her heart was beating wildly, her hands shaking with nerves, as she opened the door for both of them to enter.

Their first date had been a relaxed cup of coffee at a small cafe two days after she had heard his message. Despite having trouble believing that she was actually there, actually *on a date*, she had been reasonably calm; excited, happy, but not too nervous. The noon date had turned to mid-afternoon and they had said goodbye. Melissa had already turned down his offer of a lift, claiming that she had somewhere she needed to go. It hadn't been true, and she guessed that Michael probably knew that; she just wanted to be a little cautious. The soft way his lips had grazed against her own as they said goodbye made it clear that she hadn't offended him in the slightest, and the phone call from him the next morning to invite her for a drink confirmed that she hadn't upset him.

Carrying the coffees through to the living room, seeing him sitting on the sofa looking at the book she was currently reading, Melissa realised why she had been able to keep the bulk of her anxiety away on their first date – there had been no danger of it leading anywhere. But now, alone with him in her house, she knew exactly where she wanted the night to lead.

"Thanks." He took the offered cup from her and put it on the table next to him before turning to look at her again.

Butterflies performed daring and complicated dances in her stomach as she sat beside him, her black jeans-clad leg resting against his blue jeans-clad leg.

"What's it about?" Michael gestured towards the book next to his cup.

"It's a fantasy book; so, dragons, knights on white horses, acts of heroism, that kind of stuff." Self-consciously, she laughed softly. "A bit stupid, I know."

"Not at all. I read slashers – same stuff, just a different backdrop." He picked up his cup and took a sip, looking at her over the rim. "So, how's it feel?"

She had no idea what the non-specific question meant and she looked at him in confusion. "How does what feel?"

Laughing, his eyes dancing, he put his cup back on the table. "The tattoo. Has it healed up okay?"

"Oh!" She laughed, more comfortably. "For a moment I wondered what the hell you were talking about! Yeah, it's all healed; it looks really good."

"Have you only got the one?"

"Yeah, that was my first."

"Sounds like you're planning more."

"Paul said it's addictive. I didn't believe him."

"Now you do?"

"Yeah, now I do. How many have you got?"

Proudly, Michael grinned. "Seven."

"Seven?!" Melissa's voice rose to almost a shout. "Seriously?" Her cheeks reddened a little – but only a little. "Can I see them?"

His dark blue eyes held hers. "I'll show you mine if you show me yours."

More confident that she ever thought she could be, she smiled slyly. "I think this is a case of gentlemen first."

Moving to sit on the edge of the sofa, laughing gently, Michael began to undo the buttons on his black shirt. As he moved out of it, draping it over the back of the sofa, Melissa's eyes moved from their hungry absorbing gaze of his toned body, turning to look at the artwork that had been added to it.

Without any sense of abashment she moved closer to him and stared intently at the tattoo on his right arm. The black tribal symbols started across his shoulder, close to the base of his neck, and nearly reached the crease of his elbow. The second tattoo, this one on his shoulder, was smaller; a small skull encased in flames, with a thin-bladed dagger piercing one empty eye socket.

Gently she grasped his left hand turning it so that she could see the small black dragon that sat on the soft flesh of his inner wrist. Touching him, feeling his warm skin under hers, his pulse racing under her fingertips, she looked into his eyes. "That's three," she said, her voice soft and slightly husky.

"There's another on my back. The other three are on my legs."

She let go of his arm to allow him to turn, his back now to her. Silently, she gasped and her quivering hand stretched out to touch his back. Barely making contact, her fingers brushed across the image of the wolf, her breath stolen.

"That's incredible," she managed to whisper, moving along the lines. She traced each curve of the animal's body, feeling his hot flesh as she did. Its eyes were wide and wild, the blood that dripped from its jaws pooling on the ground beneath. She marvelled at the detail, half-expecting to feel soft fur as she traced across its body.

"Your turn," Michael said as he turned back to her.

As he had done, Melissa turned her back to him and raised her top over her head, keeping her arms in the sleeves but all of the material now in front of her. Her eyes closed as his fingers touched her back.

"Wow."

He'd moved closer and she could feel his breath in waves on her, could feel herself becoming lost in his aftershave again. She had memorised her tattoo, knew where each line fell on her skin, knew what his fingertips were touching. At the small of her back, the hilt of the sword, wrapped in fabric lengths; the cross guard holding the words 'LIVE OR DIE' in gothic script that were at waist height; the length of the thin double-edged sword that rose to a point between her shoulder blades. And it was there that his lips first pressed, causing a tingling that spread through her body. As his hands moved over her shoulders and upper arms he continued to kiss her neck, Melissa moved her head to one side so he could reach more.

She let her top glide from her arms to the floor before turning to face Michael. She slid her bare arms around his neck and met his lips with hers. It was gentle but passionate, their tongues touching softly.

Fifteen minutes later, as Melissa took his hand from her breast and led him upstairs to her bedroom, she was astounded as to how natural and familiar it felt, almost as if they were long-time lovers. And that feeling persisted as they joined together upon the bed.

Her eyes opened, her mind rising out of the sleep-induced amnesia and she immediately became aware of the heat from the naked body behind her, tight against hers. His arm was draped over her waist, his hand tucked underneath her, and she could feel the soft hair of his arm against her smooth stomach. His sleeping breath was warm against her neck, sending those exquisite vibrations through her.

Smiling, she lay there simply allowing everything to fall into place in her mind, recalling everything of the night before. When she had played it all out, she carefully slipped out of his embrace, grabbed her dressing gown and walked to the bathroom.

Hoping that the noise of the toilet flushing hadn't disturbed him, Melissa looked at her reflection in the bathroom cabinet's mirror as she washed her hands. Her hair was slightly in disarray, she looked a little tired, but the smile on her face and the sparkle in her eyes made her shine.

The sun had begun its climb and pale light filtered through the curtains, touching everything in the room. Beside the bed,

Melissa dropped her dressing gown and got back under the quilt. Immediately, his arm snaked back around her waist and his lips kissed the nape of her neck. "Morning."

"I thought you were still asleep," she said as she rolled over to lie on her other side, looking into the open eyes opposite her own.

Michael smiled sleepily. "It was lovely and warm; I woke up when the warmth left."

"Sorry," she whispered, still smiling.

"Don't be." He pulled her closer, every part of her naked body against his. "I'd rather lie next to you awake than asleep."

"Yeah?"

"Uh-huh." He kissed the tip of her nose and then her mouth. "Definitely." His hand ran up her back, tickling her briefly. "I wanted to ask you something though."

"Oh?" She moved backwards a little so she could look into his eyes a bit better.

"You don't have to answer, but…"

Melissa had an idea of where it was heading.

"Your arms? The scars?"

"I tried to kill myself." She said the words without any shame or any hesitation.

"I thought that's what it meant." He lapsed into silence, looking at her deeply; but not with pity, or morbid curiosity, just looking. Finally he smoothed a few strands of hair from her face. "Well, everyone has their own stuff to deal with, and I won't ask unless you invite me to. But, things are better for you now?"

"Yes. Lots."

"Then that's all that matters."

He pulled her close again and kissed her gently, his hands moving over her. With the sun soaring higher in the brightening sky, Melissa and Michael moved together under the sheets.

Finally, after all that had happened between them without any awkwardness, Melissa felt nervous and unsure of how to play it. But Michael took the lead and, after opening the door, turned back to her. He lay his hands on her waist and drew her to him, kissing her deeply.

"I'll call you later, Melissa."

Almost breathlessly she smiled and whispered, "Okay."

Halfway out of the door, he entered the house again to kiss her once more before leaving and walking away, smiling broadly.

Melissa closed the door and walked to the living room. Looking out of the window she watched as Michael got into his car and drove away. She sighed deeply, contentedly.

As she showered, rinsing the shampoo lather out of her hair and watching as it circled the drain, she found herself again and again picturing the tattoo that Michael had on his back, wondering if it meant something or was merely a coincidence. The picture, the meticulous details that had gone into it, had carved and burned its way into her mind and she could see it clearly with her eyes open, overlaid over everything else.

Buttoning her jeans, she stopped suddenly. "That cheat!" she said to the empty bedroom, smiling. "He never *did* show me those other three tattoos!" Laughing, she finished getting dressed.

Melissa nearly missed her footing as she hurried down the stairs, barely stopping herself from falling as she grabbed the banister. The shrill tone of the phone allowed no time for her to reflect over the close shave. She grabbed the phone.

"Hello?"

"Melissa?"

"Hi, Michael." The butterflies that had recently taken up residence in her stomach began to move restlessly as she spoke his name.

"You okay? You sound a bit out of breath."

"Yeah, I'm fine. I just ran down the stairs."

"Oh, okay." After a short pause, his voice was half-serious, half-teasing. "You know, you need to be careful, running down the stairs. You don't want to fall and hurt yourself."

"Yeah." Melissa laughed a little, his comment slightly *too* apt. "So, how are you?"

"I'm really good. I've been a bit distracted at work today, though, thinking about last night and this morning. Thinking about you."

She closed her eyes at his words, warmth building up in her, flooding into her face. "And what have you been thinking?" she asked, the teasing clear in her tone.

"What a great time I had."

"Me too. I had a really good time."

"Do you think you might want to see me again then, sometime?"

Not believing that it would have been possible for her to feel any happier than she already did, Melissa felt the warming glow increase in her heart. "I think I might be able to cope with that," she said with a laugh.

"Things seem to be getting better for you."

"I still can't believe how *much* better! I can't get over how happy I'm feeling!" Melissa was smiling; she always seemed to be smiling recently.

"I'm glad." Andrew was looking at her, also smiling, from his usual chair. She sat straighter, more self-assured than when they'd first met. Her clothes weren't as concealing either, and although she continued to wear long sleeves she no longer pulled at them, not seeming to notice the few times they rose up to show the beginnings of her scars.

"I'm even thinking about trying to look for work."

This phased Andrew a little, taking away the smallest bit of pride at her accomplishments and replacing it with worry. He sat forward a little on his seat. "Melissa, you've managed to get so far in only…what…? Five weeks? You seem so much happier in yourself, so much happier with everything around you. If you really, *truly*, feel ready to, then great. Just don't push yourself too much."

Melissa nodded. "I know how far I've come, and I've got no intention of trying to push myself too far. I'm not going to let myself go back to where I was. All I'm doing is *thinking* about looking for something – I don't even know what kind of thing I'd look for anyway."

"Fair enough. And what about the self-harming? Still no problems?"

"No, no problems." She looked at his slightly raised eyebrows. "I've had a few times when I've wanted to, when I felt like I needed to cut. But I haven't given in to it yet."

Andrew shook his head. "Don't say 'yet'. Saying 'yet' sets your mind up to eventually give in."

"Okay," she said, smiling. "I haven't given in to it."

"Better." Knowing that he was taking a risk but also that it was one that ultimately had to be taken, Andrew asked another question. "Are you ready to start talking to me about your mum, Melissa?"

The mention of her bit deeply, but Melissa smiled and took a deep, though slightly shaky, breath and started to speak.

Melissa sat in the corner of the sofa, knees tucked into her chest. She was now drained, incapable of any movement and empty of all emotion – she had made sure of being empty of emotion. Her eyes were red and puffy, the skin of her face stung with the salt of her tears, her chest hurt from the strained effort of crying. And the cut she had made on the upper side of her lower left arm screamed its colour out at her.

It didn't hurt, wasn't deep enough to have caused too much pain, but clawing the tip of the paperclip across her skin had been enough; enough to scratch the itch inside her; enough to let the blood flow and dampen the need to a bearable level. She still ached to do more, to drive the discarded metal deeper into her skin, to keep gouging at her flesh. But making that single scratch had given her the strength to rein in her compulsion; the sight of her blood let loose shocking her back to reality.

The room was dark, the cloudy night skies letting no light through the open and bare windows, shadows shrouding everything.

Thought began to filter in to Melissa as the night went on, moving past the emptiness until she had no choice but to surrender to it. Slowly she stood and made her way to the kitchen, closing her eyes at first so that there would be no temptation to even glance at the knives.

With her hands wrapped around the cup and her legs tucked up beside her, the guilt for having succumbed to her weakness began to build up but Melissa pushed it away. Andrew had warned her that guilt about it was pointless and destructive, and would ultimately lead to worse; that the only thing to do was acknowledge it, accept it, and move on from it. But freeing herself of the guilt wasn't all that easy, especially when only the morning before she had told Andrew that she hadn't given in.

It was amazing how a few hours could change things.

Talking about her mother, delving deep into the past that she had worked so hard to bury, hadn't helped. But it was not that – or, at least, not that *alone* – that had triggered her first proper spell of self-harming since her suicide attempt.

As they'd arranged, Michael and Melissa had met at the cafe after her appointment with Andrew. He'd asked her how it had gone, and had seemed glad when she told him that Andrew felt happy changing to fortnightly appointments. They'd talked for a while, and it had been really good to just be around him.

When Melissa had started back towards the table after excusing herself to go to the toilet, she'd seen Michael talking to a waitress. She had curly bleach-blonde hair, long slim legs, and a small waist. Looking at her, at the way Michael was looking at her, made all of the confidence she had built up in herself fade. Melissa knew that if she were to stand beside the blonde the plainness of her own features and figure would be too evident. And as the woman walked away and she saw the way Michael turned to watch her movements she also knew who his eyes would linger on.

Feeling ungraceful, she weaved through the other tables to join him, trying to dismiss what she had seen and the pain it had caused her, but when he looked at her Melissa was sure that he was able to see her jealousy, and that he was pleased by it.

Yet as the afternoon went on she was able to focus more on him and less on her doubts, their conversations distracting her from her own fears and insecurities.

The true trigger was what happened after they had returned to Melissa's home.

When Michael had told her about the party, Melissa felt herself divided. She wanted to say yes, wanted to go with him and meet his friends, wanted to spend the night with him there. And if he had asked for any other night she would have said yes in a heartbeat. But he was asking her to spend October thirty-first, Samhain, with him.

When she told him that she couldn't, that for her it was one of the most important nights of the year for her beliefs, he'd started to sulk. His eventual assertion that he couldn't believe that she was refusing to go to a party with him because of a stupid part of her faith made Melissa more angry than hurt. And Michael liked it even less when she asked him what the party was *for*, answering the question herself when he refused to. He only looked at the wall when she told him that his friends were planning to celebrate her 'stupid faith', only with a different name.

When he had asked her, cruelly, if she's said no because of the good-looking waitress he'd talked to earlier coldness had seeped into her, and she'd calmly but firmly told him to go. Looking shocked, Michael did as she asked, leaving Melissa to crossly pace around her living room, replaying the argument in her head; and to, in the end, sink to the floor in tears.

An hour later she had put metal to her skin.

Chapter Five

He hadn't shown any interest in any of her poems once since they'd started seeing each other, hadn't asked to see anything she'd written or even asked her what they were about, so she had no reason to hide them away; but she hid them anyway. The loose leaves of paper that she drafted her poems onto, along with the book that housed the finished work, were always put back in the box in her wardrobe. Whereas the idea of showing Andrew her poems had filled her with a nervous excitement, the idea of letting Michael read them made her far too uncomfortable; she wasn't worried about his reaction to them or his opinion of them, she just didn't want him to read them. So she put them away.

He wasn't due for another two hours, but Melissa found that she couldn't settle. She was anxious about seeing him, it was really that simple. Things had been strained between them since the argument; well, strained from Melissa's viewpoint – Michael seemed to be completely over it.

She hadn't heard from him at all on the Thursday, and had driven herself close to insanity by obsessively checking her mobile phone to see if she had received any calls or text messages, all the time telling herself that she didn't want to hear from him. She was angry with him for how he'd reacted when she had turned him down, and annoyed that he had tried to pin it onto her being jealous. She was also angry with herself for having cut, even on such a mild scale; and the guilt that she felt about that was distorting how she felt about the argument, trying to lay the blame at her door. But she *knew*, deep down underneath the false emotions, that she had handled it as tactfully as possible, that it *had not* been her that had overreacted.

As the evening changed to night her anger turned to despair at his continued silence, and the urge to cut started to creep back on to her. It happened at first without her knowledge; she looked down to see that the thumbnail of her right hand was moving in a long line, making shallow indentations on the fleshy part of her left palm, just making thin stripes that quickly disappeared. Once she noticed this she became aware of the pounding of her heart, of the desire to see the blood flowing again.

Repeatedly she told herself that she wasn't going to do it, wasn't going to give in, sometimes speaking out loud in the darkening room. In a bid to distract herself she walked in her garden, but that need followed her, resounding in her body in time to her footsteps. Back in the house, her mind having surrendered, she went to the bathroom.

The nail scissors were sharp, and the bathroom light bounced off the metal making them shine. Melissa sat on the edge of the bath and rolled her left sleeve up, the implement she had chosen held open and ready.

The scratch she had made the night before looked like a graze, an accident. She knew as she followed it that the mark she was about to make would go deeper, and it would be clear as it healed as to how it happened; it would be obvious that it was self-inflicted. She was breathing quickly, her heart hammering heavily within her chest, and when she edged the scissors closer her hand was shaking. Tears rolled down her cheeks as she fought the conflicting emotions, as her compulsion to cut fought her determination not to concede.

With a loud yell Melissa threw the unused scissors away from her, hearing the bang as they hit the tiled wall and the successive clatter as they fell into the bath.

Almost fifteen minutes later, her eyes red from crying, feeling hollowed out yet strangely content, Melissa walked back into the living room. This time when she slid open her phone it wasn't to check to see if Michael had contacted her, but so that she could turn it off. When she also unplugged the house phone from the socket, relief washed over her and she started to relax.

With the television broadcasting a sitcom and a hot toddy in her hands, curled up comfortably on the sofa, Melissa smiled. She was proud of herself; she had managed successfully to combat her self-harming. Emotionally and mentally it had been painful, but she had managed it. And now that she had done it once, it would be easier to do a second time.

She switched the phones back on and plugged them back in just before midday on Friday and, despite how good she felt about the night before, a brief knock of disappointment hit when there were no messages on her mobile. So that she wouldn't be tempted to continuously look at it, Melissa put the phone behind an ornament of a wolf on one of the shelves above the TV and left it there until it beeped just over two hours later.

The message from Michael still didn't exactly make her smile, but she did feel better having heard from him.

When he arrived at her house that evening, a box of chocolates held out to her as she opened the door, the unsure smile on his face made her unhappiness weaken, and his assertion that he'd behaved like an idiot made it easier for her to try and overlook the whole thing as unimportant.

It was only after he had left the following morning, after kissing her goodbye that Melissa realised that he hadn't actually apologised. He'd acted apologetic and regretful but had neglected specifically to say sorry. Since then, Melissa had been unable to shake the whole thing off; it was going to be difficult for her to forgive without an apology.

Now waiting, the radio in the kitchen playing quietly, she just sat and looked out at the warm autumn day. At the sound of knocking on her front door, she sighed wearily as she stood to answer it.

"Are you sure about not coming with me tomorrow to the party?"

She stopped playing with the noodles on her plate and turned to look at him. "I told you, Michael, I can't. If it had been any other day then I would have, but not tomorrow."

"Okay, that's cool. I just wanted to make sure."

He turned his attention back to the film on TV, eating his Chinese takeaway heartily, but Melissa had seen the lack of humour in his eyes before he had looked away, and couldn't ignore the tense set of his jaw. Continuing to move her food around without eating much of it, she looked at him out of the corner of her eye. He had actually believed that she would have changed her mind, and his repeated dismissal of the importance of her celebrations made her feel tired.

* * *

Melissa was smiling as she picked bits of grass and autumn leaves from her hair. Peace, happiness and contentment had devoured her as she had lain under the warm October sky, her head resting on her arms, staring up as the colours changed from blue to deep reds and oranges and then to rich purples before blackness had reigned. The weather was perfect, warm without being uncomfortable, and she walked in her T-shirt and jeans without needing anything else to cover her.

There was no ritual that she performed on Samhain, just the silent meditation and reflection as her year ended and a new one started, feeling the energy and power of the world around her and taking it into herself. Mostly what she had focussed on as she lay on the ground were the two opposing images that she believed defined the changes in herself: running across the fields, falling on to the ground, and sobbing beneath the moon; and sobbing as the scissors clattered in the bath, fear of what she had almost done turning to admiration for what she *hadn't* done. And although those acts were separated by only seven weeks, they symbolised to Melissa a life she refused to subject herself to again, and a life that she wanted to embrace.

When she showered she turned the water a little cooler than normal, letting it refresh her as it washed over her, and deciding that it was still too warm for her short pyjamas wrapped her dressing gown around her otherwise naked body.

The three candles on the table beside her lit the room with their dusky light in the dark living room, casting shadows across the walls. She ignored the blinking of the small red light on her answer phone, her stomach jumping madly. She knew that it had to be Michael, and the fact that she didn't want to hear his messages straight away left her a little confused. She thought about switching on her mobile, to check the messages that she knew she would have on that, but decided against it, for the same reason that she didn't intend to listen to her landline answer phone – she had no intention of replying or calling him until tomorrow, so the messages could wait.

The positive spirit that she had absorbed from the night outside didn't fade from her, but nonetheless it felt slightly tainted. Melissa sat on the sofa and watched the dancing shadows that moved across the walls sent by the flickering candle flames, striving to rid herself of her uncertainties; and, almost hypnotised by the rhythmic shadows, she fell asleep.

She ran through the moonlit night, lithely vaulting over the woodland obstacles, bounding around tree trunks and rocks. Her acute sense of smell was filled by the scents of the night, every plant and animal known to her. She could feel the breeze as it moved through her fur, bringing with it more exhilarating odours, and her paws pushed her along the ground at speed.

The leaves and branches from overhanging trees spasmodically forbade entrance to the moonlight, the stuttering glow throwing flickering shadows on the running form below. But the recurrent changes in light meant nothing to her; she had no problems in seeing the world around her. And there was no part of the darkened scenery that didn't enthral her soul.

Deep below the surface of hermind, the creature knew that it was dreaming; that soon the fey landscape would vanish into nothingness and she would awaken as Melissa Jade Adams, a five foot two twenty-three-year-old with green eyes and brown hair, who had recently tried to end her own life. But the knowledge was no more than a slight annoyance below the wonder that filled the wolf as it ran.

The woods ended and an open expanse of bluebells replaced it. As she leapt into the midst of the flower-ocean before her the sweet smell of the flowers and the grass that mingled with it overwhelmed her. In pure delight, the wolf lifted its muzzle to the ink-coloured sky and howled.

Her head snapped back to face the path that she had just travelled on through the trees, the fur on her body rising as another howl answered her own. In all of the time that she had run these woods and the meadows beyond, all of the years she had sought this refuge, each time in moonlight, there had never been another being.

And now, as she tasted the air, there was the presence of another wolf.

Cautiously she began to pad back towards the entrance to the woods, the sweetness of the flowers around her forgotten as her two natures began to join in the confusion. The light-hearted creature that had chased the moon's light no longer existed. The second howl that had announced the twist had summoned the girl's mind back, and she knew that there was a reason for it, had to be a reason.

Silently she moved amongst the trees again, her powerful senses leading her onwards. Leading her to that unrecognised other.

The wolf stood in a shaft of blue light, illuminating its white, brown and black fur. Its eyes blazed, and the being that would soon reclaim its human form could feel and smell the danger that emanated from it. Everything warned her not to get too close, to just turn tail and run from the creature before her.

Just as she was about to – to back away and keep going – she saw something else. Behind the wolf with the blazing eyes stood a third wolf, but she could see nothing else; it stood completely in the shadows of a large tree, everything concealed, merely a silhouette. But she wanted to go to it, to stride briskly past the dangerous creature and move alongside the other one. To lose herself in its presence.

Feeling her desire take control of her senses she edged a little nearer. But the wolf that stood in front barred its sharp teeth and growled low, deep in its throat, turning slightly to the side to prevent any access.

Confusion started to rain on the human part of the creature and she stopped her approach. There was no safe way for her to reach that unseen other, not without suffering great harm.

Melissa knew that she would soon wake, but she didn't want to spend the last moments in the world she had created staring into those deadly eyes. With a last longing glance at that dark shape, the female wolf bolted back the way she had come, easily avoiding the pieces of woodland debris, blue light fluttering over her again, trying to lose herself in the run.

The blue light of the moon changed to the pale yellow glow of the candles as Melissa opened her eyes, tentatively at first to give herself time to adjust to the brightness.

She longed to delve into the meaning of her dream, to try to decipher what it all represented. But, stifling a yawn, Melissa pinched out the three still-flickering flames and went to bed, ignoring the consistently flashing answer phone light.

* * *

"So, how was your Samhain?" As he looked at her, Andrew saw the rush of conflicting emotions that fluttered in her green eyes and the way her smile stuttered a little before holding.

"A little strange." She had promised herself that she would be honest and completely truthful with Andrew – he was, after all, there to help her, and anything else would be detrimental to everything she'd managed to achieve. "Things have been a little strange."

"Strange how? Does 'things' include Michael?"

"Yeah, it includes Michael." Looking at the cloudy sky through the window she smiled. Only a week into November the temperature had dropped drastically, and it looked as though she would have the opportunity in the next few hours to walk once more in the rain.

"After our appointment the other week Michael and I had an argument. I ended up self-harming." Despite her resolution not to allow herself to feel guilty, Melissa was unable to stop the colour bleeding into her cheeks.

"How badly?"

She shook her head. "Not bad. I used a paperclip and just scratched the surface of the skin on my arm. I *did* come close to cutting properly the day after; I actually had the scissors held near to the skin, but I stopped myself from doing it – which wasn't easy!"

"No, it wouldn't be." He paused for a moment, looking at her carefully. "But, without wanting this to sound patronising, Melissa, I'm really proud of you. To only harm a little, and then to *stop* yourself when you have the compulsion to do some serious damage…it's a really good sign."

She grinned. "Thank you. I'm proud of myself, too. Made me realise that I can fight it, even if it's not always completely."

"What did you argue about?"

"It started as nothing and then just escalated into a bigger nothing. It's too stupid to go into."

"Okay. So you made up?"

"Yeah, sorted it out, more or less. He went to a Halloween party – that's actually one of the things we argued about; he wanted me to go, and was a little upset when I told him I couldn't.

"When I came in after my Samhain stuff, there were loads of messages on my answer phone, and I didn't even bother listening to them. I fell asleep and had a bit of a weird dream."

"Weird?"

She shook her head gently. "It's a dream I've had all my life, but this time there was a new element to it. I know what it means, what it indicates. I've just got to reconcile myself with the facts of it."

"Okay. When did you check your messages?"

"The next morning."

"What were they like?"

Melissa sighed heavily. "The first couple on my house phone weren't too bad – just 'wish you were here' kind of messages. Then he started to get an edge to his voice; getting a little drunk as well. The messages he sent to my mobile, texts for the most part, were worse. He was getting pissed off that I wasn't answering his calls or replying to his texts."

"That's a little unfair." Andrew looked at her steadily, wondering how far to push this. "Just because you had other things to do…"

Melissa smiled. "It was *very* unfair. It's not like I agreed to go and then cancelled on him." Mentally she shook off the feelings that his messages had caused her to go through. "Anyway, I sent him a text that afternoon, apologising for not replying sooner."

"And?"

"I didn't hear from him until Saturday."

"He was sulking?"

"Yeah, I think so. He said he'd just been busy, but it felt too much like he was playing games. You know, 'You ignored me, so I'll ignore you'."

"That's a bit…" Andrew paused, trying to find a suitable word that wouldn't cause too much offence.

"Sad? Pathetic? Childish?" Melissa offered with a grin. She watched him nod. "Don't worry, those words came easily to *my* mind at the time."

"What happened on Saturday?"

"He knocked on my door with a bunch of flowers and a box of chocolates; I guess it was his way of apologising for ignoring me on the Thursday."

What Melissa *didn't* feel able to tell him regardless of her promise to be one hundred per cent truthful was that she thought it was his way of apologising for something else, something that he wasn't able to admit to her. The suspicious-looking red bruise-type marks on his chest and lower neck as they lay in bed that evening left her in no doubt about what else he had been saying sorry for.

She pushed her trolley through the aisles, trying not to let herself get annoyed as people knocked into her and pushed past her. She had no idea why it was so busy; Wednesday afternoons were usually quiet, which is why she liked to do her shopping then.

She had left her appointment with Andrew having decided something. It had been a long time since she had planned an evening of relaxation and indulgence; and today, with the clouds heavy but seemingly unwilling to share the rain, Melissa believed it would be a perfect night to treat herself.

The list of DVDs to watch was compiled in her head, there was a selection of dips and crisps in her trolley, and all that was left to do was chose a bottle of wine and she'd be all set.

The distraction of pre-planning her evening was working; although there was no way for her *not* to be aware of the rude and impatient shoppers that still collided with her trolley and with her, the thought of the night ahead made them all insignificant.

She didn't take long to pick out a decent bottle of rosé wine – she wasn't a big drinker and tended to stick with what she knew, and had just placed it with the rest of her shopping when a hand tapped her shoulder.

"Hi, Mellie."

Every good feeling she had, and had experienced since starting therapy, were torn from her heart's grasp. The woman she had had no contact with, whom she had changed her phone number in order to avoid, was standing before her; and looked a mess.

"Hi, Mum." Melissa was unable to prevent the grimace as she glanced in to her mother's trolley and saw the half-dozen bottles of vodka and Scotch.

They stood in silence, her mother's bloodshot eyes straining to focus on her, while Melissa resolutely looked everywhere but at the woman in front of her.

"Mellie—"

Furiously, she looked at her mum. "*Don't ever* call me that!" Noting the way that she didn't look even slightly perturbed by the change of tone, Melissa took hold of her trolley and steered it towards the checkouts. The plans for the evening no longer currently mattered; all she wanted now was to get the hell out of the shop – as quickly as possible.

Chapter Six

She sat crying on the wet ground, rain hammering on her shivering form. She wrapped her arms around her body but they did nothing to warm her. She trained her on the red lines that had seeped through the jeans from the thighs beneath, wishing that she had cleaned and dressed the cuts before going outside; if the blood dried before she could get the jeans off it would hurt like mad – and she had caused herself enough pain.

There had been no trigger; nothing on which she could pin her desire to cut. Although her mind offered one excuse, there was no way that simply not being able to see the full moon could account for her picking up the nail scissors.

As she had held them her brain threw at her, as it had done each and every time since, the memory of her throwing the scissors away, of successfully fighting it. But, angry at the thought for trying to prevent it from happening, she had forcibly pushed it aside. And when, in a last-ditch attempt, her mind had shown her an image of her tattoo, of the words etched in to her skin, this just seemed to spur her on – she longed to etch more on her flesh.

Melissa had sliced her skin rapidly, each cut she added sending streaks of red lightning through her body to strike at her soul. When she stopped and the pleasure she felt as she watched the blood flow drained away, she started to tremble and quickly pulled her jeans back on.

Hoping that the sky had cleared, taking the rain with it, she rushed into her garden. The guilt of cutting and the emptiness that followed, needed an antidote; she needed to look at the moon, needed to feel its light bleed back in to her heart. Staring up as the rain hit her face, with not even an echo of the moon's glow penetrating the thick clouds, Melissa felt denied.

Hollowed out and feeling more alone that she had in a long

time, she lowered her head, scrambled ungracefully to her feet and almost hobbled back inside. Grimacing, she peeled her wet trousers off. The congealed blood, choosing to stay with the fabric, forced the cuts opened again and she began to bleed. In her bedroom she stripped the rest of the sodden clothes off and left them in a wet pile on the floor. She wandered into the bathroom, securing her dressing gown with the belt as she went.

Her eyes were sore from crying and they felt heavier as they looked at the scissors on the edge of the bath, the blades still open and marked with the blood. Too weary to even wipe the metal clean, Melissa proceeded to clean and dress the reopened cuts on her thighs, wishing to just collapse onto her bed; but she knew that if she didn't at least cover the wounds then she'd have to rip her bed sheets from her skin in the morning.

Finally Melissa crawled into her bed, but sleep took a long time to visit – and when it did, she was lost in her dreams.

Panting she ran along beside the stream, following it as it flowed onwards. The pungent odour clawed enticingly at her keen nose, almost trickling like water down her throat. The woods she moved through, as familiar to her as breathing, were dark and foreboding, the usually light air filled with dense oppression. As much as she tried to ignore those instincts of something not right, to concentrate on the inviting stream beside her, those feelings pressed down on her.

A soft bark from the far bank brought her to a sudden stop. Despite the strength of her eyes, how clear the night-engulfed world appeared to her, the wolf that stood on the other side of the stream appeared as simply a mass of blackness against a dark backdrop. But she could smell him; could smell gentleness and protection and peace.

She barked a reply, a greeting, and began to step closer to the incline, meaning to stride through the stream to him. A growl beside her stopped her steps and the scent of the wolf with the blazing eyes filled her nostrils. It moved in front of her, still growling, once again preventing her from going to the other.

Passion surged through her, wild ferocity and violence, and a trembling started in her limbs. Shaking with the suppression of her anger she bared her own teeth, feeling the power hidden in her jaws. When the male wolf tried to make her move backwards away from the stream her restraint broke and she lunged forwards, sinking her teeth into his flank. He yelped loudly and darted away, looking at her mistrustfully.

With his blood on her tongue, she waited until he had disappeared back into the cover of the trees before turning back to look across the stream. Although that indistinct creature was still in sight it had retreated away from her. Determinedly she traced her way down the slope of the stream.

The closer she got to the water the more it distracted her from everything else. As it had when she had run with it, the scent of the waters filled her. Her paws splashed sending ripples away from her, and pain travelled up her legs and into her soul.

Melissa was thrown back into the wolf's body, no longer purely an animal, the meaning of her dream becoming clearer to her. The water wasn't water – she had known that as she'd followed it. The blood that ran through the woods was hers, and the pain that it brought was hers. In her peripheral vision she could see that the other wolf had returned to stand at the edge of the stream, watching her silently, waiting for her to join him now that the obstacle had been removed. But she couldn't look at him, didn't want to – she was wading in the thick red waters and it was all she cared about.

When its current started to grow stronger, sweeping her off her feet, the wolf that housed the girl ignored all other desires and fears; and just let herself drown in the agonising pleasure of her self-harm.

The taste of blood was still in her mouth when she woke up the next morning, and pain still echoed in her mind. She lay on her back and stared across at the dull light that illuminated the curtains. Jumbled images from her life pushed inside her head, trying to be noticed and seen, negotiating a few hours of peace with a promise to analyse them later.

Her dressing gown had come undone during the night, exposing her as she lifted back the covers. Forgetting the actions of the previous night, Melissa swung her legs out of bed without a care, the ache that moved through her making her wince.

Eyes closed, she prepared herself before looking at her uncovered legs. Two of the long plasters had completely soaked through, had left impressions on the bed sheets, and the area around them was discoloured with bruises. Timidly she began to peel the coverings from her cuts, feeling the skin pulled and causing one of the cuts that had healed to crack open again. The ones that had bled through their plasters still wept, one badly, and she knew that she would have to be careful to make sure that it didn't become infected.

The shower ran hot and the stinging caused as the water ran across her thighs brought tears to her eyes. She washed her hair, working her fingers through the many tangles that had appeared overnight. Tentatively she washed her body, trying to find a balance between gentleness and thoroughness.

After patting herself dry she applied antiseptic cream to the self-inflicted gashes before dressing them again.

Her pain and sadness due to her actions the night before lessened somewhat when she was dressed and with a hot drink in her hand. Standing in the kitchen, leaning against the kitchen side, she looked out over her garden. The rain had turned to drizzle and it drained the colour from the world, leaving it empty.

Those nagging thoughts began to clamour for attention again, yet Melissa would not be rushed. There was a vague notion forming in her mind, an idea of how to work out what had caused her to harm herself so badly, what had triggered her to give in to such extremity. But she wouldn't allow it to rise to the top of her mind unformed; so she stood and drank her tea while she looked at the emptiness of the world outside.

The text message she received from Michael was pleasant, an invitation for her to spend Saturday afternoon with him. But it arrived just as she was going upstairs to her spare room, and she didn't want to be distracted. Knowing that her reply would be viewed in the wrong way but in too much of a rush, she told him that she was busy and that she'd speak to him later. Then she threw the phone onto the sofa and continued with what she was doing.

Her spare room was a mass of organised clutter. Two large bookcases housed an assortment of novels, poetry compilations and a fair number of books concerning mental health – mainly depression and self-harm. There were also a dozen books on paganism and spirituality. In a box file on the bottom shelf of one of the bookcases was a selection of soft-backed, hard-backed and spiral-bound notepads.

She took one of the smaller pads downstairs and sat on the sofa, but she didn't feel right. She was too comfortable, too unfocussed, so she sat at the dining table.

One thing that Melissa had never been able to criticise herself for, even when she'd tried, was her ability to compile the facts and organise them, to sort and catalogue them; to analyse herself, her actions and her motives. Her instincts and intuitions about her dreams were always accurate, and she was always able to decipher the important messages that were encrypted there.

On the first page of the book, in small elegant writing, she started to make a list of the vivid parts of her dreams, the parts that seemed more real, more *there,* than the background noise of it.

After looking at the list she had compiled, Melissa closed her eyes and let her mind focus on them, keeping her breathing slow and steady, while she waited for the explanations for each to present themselves.

She had no idea how long she had stayed there with her eyes closed, but it took a little while to adjust to looking at the almost blinding white paper once her eyes had reopened. With the reasons down on paper she looked over it.

The wolf with the blazing eyes – Michael
The unseen wolf – an unknown person
The stream of blood – my self-harm
Letting myself drown in the stream – my willingness to let my self-harm stop me from achieving anything

On another page she started a new section, giving it a heading, which she underlined.

Self-Harm Triggers

She stared at those words, tapping her pen against the pad of paper. Even now her mind was trying to shy away from the subject, protecting her right to harm from the rationalisations that could possibly bring it to an end. Gathering her will, conjuring the image of the scissors thrown with force, she looked at the paper with an almost hostile focus.

Melissa read the heading again, and immediately wrote the word 'Mum' underneath. Feeling almost as if she'd reached the summit of a particularly steep and treacherous mountain, she breathed out the air from her lungs that she hadn't been aware of holding.

Before she could hesitate, she wrote another word underneath the first and underlined it briskly. Michael's name seemed to glare accusingly up at her.

Sitting back in the chair, feeling the rigid hardness of the frame against her back, she looked at the list, her forehead creased. Doodling at the top of the page, drawing squares and rectangles and giving them depth by adding more lines, forcing them into 3D, Melissa looked at what she had written.

Slowly, with understanding and purpose, she moved herself

forwards and wrote again. Beneath all the rest, in huge capital letters that took up four lines, Melissa marked an 'M' followed by an 'E'. Sadness crept in on her as she looked at it, as she swept three lines underneath, as she enclosed it within a circle.

Her mind had emptied of thoughts as her fingers released their grip on the pen, laying it softly on the table beside the pad of paper that now screamed a new truth at her.

"Smoke..." she whispered as she moved from the table, the numbness following her into the kitchen, her hands automatically taking over to make her another drink.

Shadowing her stance of earlier, she looked out once more at the slow but steady drizzle that still fell from the clouds. Distantly she was able to feel the heat from her cup of coffee, could feel the kitchen side against the small of her back.

Her mind whimpered, pleading for a reprieve, a short escape, from the breakthrough that threatened to break through the barriers erected so long ago. Tremors began as she fought; wrestling with what she had started.

The trembling subsided when she decided to give herself a break, to confront it again at another time, and the smoke in her mind evaporated to let the world shift back into focus.

Tired and heavy, she retrieved her phone, preparing herself to face the music.

Chapter Seven

"Anyway, they're all healed up. I think three of them are going to scar though, one quite badly."

Andrew continued to sit back in his chair, looking relaxed. Except for the deep concern in his eyes, he looked relaxed. "That was two days after our last appointment?" He watched her nod. "Any other episodes since?"

Melissa still felt devastated by the level of disappointment that had flitted across his face as she'd first told him. As he asked that question she felt worse, and more so as she answered, "I've had a couple." She flushed a little in the face. "Four others since that one."

"But not as bad?" His hand was near his face, his thumb resting under his chin and his index finger laying against his lips.

"No. None as bad as that."

He regarded her quietly for a moment before dropping his hand back to his lap. "Where did you cut?"

The sleeves of her soft blue shirt rolled up easily to her elbows. On the backs of both arms networks of thin shallow cuts crossed back and forth, most little more than rows of fresher skin where scabs had formerly sat.

Andrew struggled to remain composed as he saw them. They weren't too extreme, he had seen deeper and more complicated cuts on several other of his patients, but the amount shocked him. Her arms looked as if an insane prisoner had decided to mark out the years held captive on skin rather than mark the walls. But despite his composure, he was unable to prevent himself from uttering softly. "Christ."

Her instinct was to immediately cover her arms again, hiding the evidence of what she'd done beneath the soft material, but she fought against the impulse. If there was anywhere where she shouldn't have to hide it, if there was any*one* that she shouldn't have to hide it from, it was here with Andrew. So despite how uncomfortable she felt with her arms showing, and the way that Andrew's eyes kept repeatedly working over the latticework of her injuries, Melissa defied it all and left her sleeves rolled up.

"I know how bad it is."

His eyes ripped away to meet hers.

"I know how bad these are, and I know how bad the ones on my legs are. I also know that it won't be the last time I harm myself."

When Andrew sat forward and opened his mouth to object, to start arguing his case about defeatist attitudes, Melissa overruled him. "Let me finish."

In compliance, he sat back and waited, now smiling slightly.

Melissa also smiled but her eyes remained serious. "It *won't* be the last time I ever take something to my skin. Admitting that doesn't mean that I'm giving up, or setting myself up, in advance, to fail; it just means I'm being honest. There *will* be times when I'm not strong enough to fight it, but there will also be times when I *am* able to – and I plan that the latter will outweigh the former."

Impressed with the compelling way she was expressing herself, he continued to smile silently.

"In a way, it's better for me that I *did* cut to such extremity." Knowing that he was looking at her puzzled, Melissa reached into her bag beside her and brought out her notebook. She didn't open it; she simply held it in her hands, feeling the strength of herself in its pages.

"After I slashed my legs, the morning after, the sheer depth of confusion of guilt and anger at myself and the pain of it all –" a deep breath brought back some control – "it forced me to work through some things; about a lot of different stuff, but mainly about why I do what I do."

Melissa's grip tightened on the notebook that she had been writing in, added to in small surges almost every day since making her first entries. "Some of it is dream interpretations; analysing the aspects that seem important to my subconscious. But most of it is about my self-harm triggers."

"And what have you come to understand?"

Melissa smiled, almost sardonically. "That I can try and pin the blame on all the small stuff, like not being able to see the full moon when I need to feel its light, or having a bad dream. And I can try and lay the blame on the bigger stuff, like stress over my mum, or arguing with Michael. But in the end, it's all caused by the same one thing."

"What is that same one thing, Melissa?"

She stared into the eyes behind those glasses, her eyebrows raised slightly. "Me."

Intrigued by her simple answer, he sat up a little straighter in the chair. "You?"

Smiling more genuinely, she nodded. "Me." She dropped the notepad on her lap and put her hands on top. "I can make all the excuses I want. I can put the blame everywhere else. But it all comes down to me, and how I deal with everything.

"I always feel strong when I manage to push away the need to cut, but I know it's not a weakness when I do. I *feel* weak when I do, I feel like I've lost the battle."

She was contradicting herself, her thoughts and self-discoveries seemed too jumbled as they came out of her mouth. More collected, she tried again.

"The reason that I cut, the reason I've *always* cut, isn't about anything else, isn't about things that happen to me or things that people *do* to me. If it were, everyone who had gone through the same kind of thing would be dealing with it in exactly the same way as I do. It's not even about how I react to things, not really. It's about me feeling that I'm not in control.

"After I wrote 'ME' in the list for my self-harm, it's like I awoke a more insightful part; as little as I liked it, I was able to figure things out a bit more."

"And the 'insightful you' told you what?"

Sighing, feeling on the verge of tears, she looked down at her arms. "I've been lying to myself. I started feeling happier, started to feel that things were coming together and that my life was finally finding some kind of direction, and I just stopped. I just stopped trying to improve more, to make things even better. I just started to let things ride out without trying."

"Melissa—"

"I tried killing myself!" she said in a near shout, startling Andrew back into silence. "Three months ago I cut my wrists! I used a knife to slit my wrists and I lay down on my kitchen floor, watching the blood leaving my body, and I wanted to die! How the fuck could that possibly all be sorted out in just three months?!"

Tears trickled down her cheeks and she angrily wiped them away. "I tried being too happy too soon. I tried letting a little bit of good feeling eradicate all the issues that I still need to get through. And I realised that it doesn't work that way! It *can't*!"

"It doesn't mean you can't be happy though."

She wiped the tears away again, this time a little more gently. "I know. But I think – no, I'm *sure* – that I started pinning all my happiness on outside influences. When what I really need to do is be happy *first*, instead of searching for reasons to be." She looked questioningly at Andrew. "Does that make any kind of sense?"

"It makes *all* kinds of sense. So what's your next move? What do you do now?"

After dropping her notes back into her bag, Melissa looked at the grey light outside. Winter had seemed to hit instantly with the arrival of November, and the last three weeks had brought a bitter cold along with the rain clouds. The heat of the autumn seemed like a faded photograph to her now, although she knew that her mood was also partly responsible for that.

"I've been thinking about that since I started writing my

notes." She swept her gaze back to her psychiatrist. "Sometimes vaguely, but sometimes very intensely."

Andrew looked at her studiously, puzzled at the complexity of the smile that was forming on her face. There were so many emotions in the soft curves of her lips: sadness, resignation, soft strength, and an almost reluctant happiness. Looking at that smile seemed to make his temples throb.

"I need to find a place for myself in the world, some kind of structure in my life that I can lean on. I know I'm not ready to try and make a career again yet, and I'm *sure* that I don't want to work as a PA again – I can't cope with that level of stress and pressure anymore. But I need to do *something*. Even if it's stacking shelves, or answering phones; I don't care. I just need to find some routine instead of wandering aimlessly through my days, doing nothing that's worth anything."

"That sounds like the right thing."

"I'm also going to finish things with Michael."

Andrew couldn't help but feel relieved; the relationship had happened much too soon, before she had been ready. He noted again the reluctant happiness in her smile again. "You don't seem all that distraught about the idea."

"I *do* like him, a lot. I like being around him. I enjoy the closeness I feel with him a lot of the time. I like lying in bed with the warmth of someone else beside me. But I'm not ready to be with him, or anyone. When I said I was going to finish things with him, I don't know if it will be just until I get things sorted out or if it'll be for good." She chuckled softly for a second. "But not knowing that just proves that I'm not sure enough to keep things going."

"But for now it's over?"

Even Melissa was aware of the sudden drop of her smile. "No, not yet." She sighed. "It's his birthday next Wednesday. One week today. I can't mar that for him."

"Putting it off won't make it any better, Melissa. For you or for him."

"I know." She stared deeply at him. "But I just can't. Not until after."

He understood her reasons. "Okay. So you want to work on things a bit more? Work through some more of your past?"

With the evidence of just shed tears still on her cheeks, Melissa smiled wearily. "'Want' may be the wrong word. But, yeah, I do think we should."

He flicked through the folder with her name on the outside and found the page on which he had made his last observations. "We left off last time talking about what happened when you were seven. You ready to keep going?"

The familiar ache settling within every part of her, Melissa closed her eyes and drew in a long, deep breath before opening her mouth to continue with the agonising story of her life.

She sat on her knees in front of the wardrobe, the doors wide open, staring at what sat inside. Her hands rested on her thighs and neither one of them would obey her commands to reach forward once more. They remained stationary, insurgent, unresponsive. And when she decided to forget her 'bright' idea and just get up and close the doors, she discovered that her legs had joined the rebellion, and she couldn't stand. Nor could she look away from the box that screamed its compelling whisper at her. Melissa had turned to marble, frozen by the prospects of seeing the contents.

Gathering all of the will that she could find inside herself, Melissa managed to close her eyes, blocking the view from her sight. Squinting, unable to see anything except a red-tinged darkness, she found that she was able to persuade her hands to reach out. Her fingertips brushed against the cardboard of the box that normally was trapped safely beneath another, and she cringed. She started to shake and agonised tears forced their way out of her eyes.

She knew that she had to do it; she knew that someday she was going to have to open the box and confront the reminders of a life that she had tried, so unsuccessfully, to forget.

Melissa crumpled back, her fingers losing contact with the still-screaming box, a whimper issuing from her throat.

She knew that the confrontation was imminent; but it wouldn't be today.

"How'd it go today?"

Melissa felt wearied at the interest and evident good mood in his voice, guilt fluttering around her like mischievous butterflies. "It was good. Intense."

Michael's voice dropped the enthusiasm a little. The concern that replaced it made those butterflies of hers more energetic.

"Are you okay?"

"Tired." She chastised herself for her attitude towards him. If she really wasn't going to end things with him for a week then she wasn't going to make him miserable for the entire time. She tried to sound a little more cheerful. "I'm sorry, Michael, I don't mean to be off. Like I said, the session was really intense and involved. I feel totally drained."

"Want a massage?"

Melissa was able to picture the seductive glint that would be in his eyes at the suggestion and smiled, genuinely. "As lovely as that sounds, I think I just need to crash tonight. Will that still be on offer tomorrow?"

"Most definitely!"

He sounded a little disappointed but not annoyed, which at least lessened some of the guilt. "Good."

They spoke for a few minutes longer before saying goodbye. With her hands still setting the receiver down she considered trying once more to open the box in her wardrobe, but immediately pushed the notion aside. Just the fact that she had tried earlier meant so much. To try once more only to fail again might be too much for her to take. And besides, Melissa believed that she had tortured herself with her past enough for one day.

There was no beginning – there never was. She always awoke in her wolf form running, she never had to make that first motion to start her body moving forwards. The girl would close her eyes while stationary and the wolf would open its eyes with paws striking the ground in fast procession.

The wolf sprinted like a bullet through the dark night but slowed gently to a stop, tongue lolling out as she panted, tasting the air.

The night had never been so dark before. When she lifted her muzzle to bay at the sky, no moon shone its light upon her fur; no stars sparkled in the velvet blackness. The clouds were dense and full of warning, the purple in them edgedwith a promise of rain. Now that her sharp eyes had noted the coming storm, the wolf could allow itself to feel the energy that surged through the air all around her. The night was charged with electricity, causing the creatures that occupied the forest to tingle in anticipation. The wolf could feel it from the centre of her spine to the tips of her fur.

Restlessly she paced back and forth, not giving in to the urge to run and leap. It wasn't time, the moment wasn't quite right yet. She knew that with the same instinct that told her that when the storm above her hit it would do so in an explosion.

As if on cue, the clouds burst open, the rain teeming down in a rush. As it stuck the she-wolf she howled, let the tension snap and sprinted forwards.

The ground quickly became sodden, the rain coming too fast and heavy for the earth to be able to absorb it. The air vibrated as the storm grew stronger. Light flashed everywhere, followed instantly by a deafening crash of thunder.

The wolf stopped running, yelping in shock, and slunk low to the ground, forcing her belly to push into the mud, her ears lying flat. Once she was sure that another flash of lightning wasn't going to immediately brighten the sky, the wolf rose and started to run again, gaining momentum steadily until she was once again almost a blur in the dark.

She caught the pungent scent and fled towards it, breathing it deep into her lungs, savouring every part of it. It grew in her flaring nostrils as she got closer, the metallic taste taking up residence in the lining of her throat. It burned, filling her with a desire that also blazed.

The red stream had devoured the riverbanks, had spilled its waters onto the ground beside, turning the earth the deep, rich colour of rust.

The she-wolf stopped on the outside of the river-absorbed earth, her paws an inch from the reddened ground. She lowered her muzzle and salaciously lapped up a few drops. A low growl that sounded very close to a pleasurable moan, escaped her throat as shivers of delectable agony coursed through her, her belly on fire.

With a frightened yelp she skittered backwards, eyeing the still-swelling river mistrustfully. A memory of drowning in the river, of the overwhelming agony that she had allowed to swallow her, rose in her mind. She longed to jump in again, to let the surrender take her over once more, to let the pain sate her. But beneath the hunger, she knew that it wasn't what she really wanted; she craved *it, but* wanted *something different.*

Taking flight, she was running blind. The rain pounded everywhere, even the leaf-clothed trees offered no respite from the torrential rain, and it obscured her vision. She had to rely on her sense of smell to guide her onwards.

Then the rain stopped. One second the rain attacked everything, and the next, not a single drop fell from the sky. The wolf shook herself to rid her fur of the water that clung to it and was more than a little bewildered when there was nothing to lose: her fur was dry. When she turned to look behind her, the trail she had made was also free of any moisture, the ground almost parched.

The wolf turned in a circle as if chasing her tail, muzzle lifted slightly as she tested the air. The scents were strange to her; the area she now stood in was new to her, the territory unmarked by any animal. Suddenly scared, she wanted to turn tail and run, run back to the world she knew, the world where familiar and comforting scents filled the air.

She didn't care if that meant having to go back into the storm, didn't care if it meant going back to that deadly inviting stream. Going back also meant falling back into the comfort of what she knew, the certainty of what lay behind each tree worth the sacrifice of escape from the destructive storm.

This was a new agony for her. As she continued to turn in a tight circle, she felt the pain of indecision. And cursed, in her lupine way, the fragility of her human element, the complexity of the choices that should have been easy to decide between.

Only when a soft bark alerted her was the she-wolf aware of the presence of the two familiar male wolves, and she snarled in anger at herself – she should have sniffed them out. Turning her back on the path she had followed, turning away from the storm and what she knew, she found herself facing another path.

And it was a true path, a clear way through the forest. The trees appeared to have almost jumped aside to allow the unobstructed and uncluttered track to have precedence over all else. But although the pathway was clear, the start of it was not. The two wolves, enemies to each other on her last two visits to this forest-world, now stood side by side, verging on a companionable truce. The one with the blazing eyes still held its former air of malice as it glared at her; and the other remained a solid block of shadow.

The wolf that was the instinctual and intuitional aspect of Melissa strode cautiously but determinedly to the head of the path. There was only a slight surprise when both wolves stepped aside, the blazing-eyed wolf to the left and the unseen wolf to the right, leaving the way open.

A shiver of excitement tingled through her as her paws touched the beginning of the path; and she was in motion.

Running faster than she had ever before been capable of, her paws hitting the ground in beautiful dance, she drove herself up the clearing. Exhilaration rushed through her soul at the prospect of what lay at the other end.

Melissa woke with a start, her heart hammering furiously

beneath her breast, her breath matching the beats. The exhilaration she had felt in her wolf form had followed her out of her dreams and into the real world. She felt as though she could do anything.

After glancing once at the alarm clock, ignoring the illuminated numbers on its front, she laced her hands and rested her head on them. Looking contentedly up at the ceiling, at the mass of dark grey that would become white when the sun rose, she decided that she had too much energy to just lie in bed longer; that despite five twenty-three being *far* too early for her to get up, she would be unable to wait the time away.

The residue of her dream, the invigoration and euphoria that had followed her out into the waking world didn't subside as she threw her covers back and leapt from the bed. Nor did it subside as she showered, actually humming a snatch of a pop song that she hadn't heard in months.

Clad in her long black T-shirt that almost met her knees, her wet hair lying flat against her back, she still hummed that song as she began to make herself a coffee. Occasional lines of lyrics burst from her lips, her hips swaying as she moved in time to the music in her head. Before the kettle could even finish boiling, the repetition of the same tune playing over and over began to grate, and she switched on the radio in her kitchen to drive it out of her head.

She'd done it before she realised what she was doing, and her mood fell a little, her hand stopping briefly in mid-air before dropping back to her side. Melissa stared at the radio that she had avoided using since the night she had tried taking her life, looking at it in a way that suggested that it was some kind of alien artefact, or some hitherto unidentified species.

The volume was low, but when a song replaced the DJ's chatter she was able to hear it. It was just another song, one she had heard many times before, but it summoned back the positive feelings she had woken with. Smiling, she reached out again and cranked up the volume, letting the steady thump of bass work through her body. Swaying again – but still not giving in completely and actually dancing – and singing in a loud not unpleasant voice, she waited for the kettle to finish heating the water then made her drink.

It would have been impossible for her to simply sit and have her drink; she was far too restless. Instead she moved around her kitchen and living room, still not quite giving in to the urge to dance to the music that pounded through the house.

Rather than dwindling as the clock ticked onwards, the zeal ravenously continued to demand her movement. Feeling like she would go crazy if she didn't concede, Melissa quickly dressed in jeans and a white T-shirt, throwing a thick, hooded fleece jumper on top, and left the house.

It was dark and bitterly cold, but she didn't care. For a moment she considered driving somewhere, maybe to the woodlands that she used to frequent, but tossed that idea aside. The woods that she used to love to visit were part of a nature reserve, and in the winter they weren't open constantly. And even if they had been, she wouldn't have trusted herself to drive for three quarters of an hour; there was too much energy coursing through her veins alongside her blood, and the temptation to speed would become too much to ignore on roads that, given the early hour, would be close to deserted. No, better to just walk.

It wasn't a gently stroll, either. Her spirit demanded that she move fast, the blood thundering through her body and pushing her further. By the time she reached the main roads, illuminated a dusky orange by the streetlamps, Melissa was sweating and, despite the cold, she was forced to remove her jumper, tying it around her waist to keep her swinging arms free of restrictions.

There was no destination in her mind, no place that she had set out for, nowhere she specifically wanted to go; she was just content to walk through the slowly lightening world. She passed a few people – early shift workers and a couple of kids on paper rounds – but mostly the streets were free of any others.

Just before half past seven, Melissa walked back into her house. She kicked her trainers off, removing the jumper from her waist as she walked into the living room and, exhausted, collapsed onto the sofa, laughing breathlessly. Her legs ached, the muscles tense and throbbing, her face and arms were flushed red, and sweat ran down her face in rivulets. She knew that the shower she had already had that morning had been completely pointless; she knew that she was going to have to repeat it. She laughed again as she thought about trekking upstairs. She'd have to repeat the shower once she was actually *capable* of reaching it!

Lying on the sofa three hours later, hair almost dry, foot tapping away to the heavy bass of the song that currently played, she put down the book she was reading. Looking at her phone that had just beeped for her attention, she smiled happily when she saw that the message was from Michael. She didn't think anything would be able to spoil her mood today.

Chapter Eight

She wanted to. God, how much she wanted to. The knife that she had taken from the kitchen and placed onto the dining table screeched for her full attention, for her to pick it up and put it to use. She had put it there on purpose, put it there so that she would be forced to look at it. It wasn't the memory of throwing the scissors away that was stopping her from wrapping her fingers around its handle; it wasn't the permanent image in her mind of her tattoo that stopped her either. It was her dream.

The dream of fighting the urge to jump into the blood river, of escaping the storm, of finding a new path, had played in her head every night since the first time. Without fail, the night had summoned that dream to her, and she awoke each day feeling that bit stronger and more elated, more optimistic.

And it was this that restrained her hands, that kept the tears from forming behind her eyes.

Andrew had been right – she should have finished with Michael when she'd first decided to; it would have saved a lot of grief.

Michael had been pleased by his birthday present, had grinned widely when he'd unwrapped the gift to see the new novel by his favourite author, and had kissed her a passionate 'thank you'. After an appreciative look up and down at the way she looked, they'd left for the party.

It was the first time she'd met any of his friends and knowing that she was going to be thrown in amongst *all* of them at the same time left her feeling more than a little anxious. Michael had helped with her nerves a little, repeating over and over in the car just how much they were all going to love her.

Melissa closed her eyes, momentarily killing her view of the knife in front of her. She knew that it was a risky thing to do, but also knew that it was a test that she needed to take. Steadying herself against the humiliation and pain that she was about to relive, she allowed the night to play out in her head, wiping away the few tears that managed to escape without any anger at herself for allowing them out.

Enthusiastic cheers, many of them alcohol-fuelled, had greeted them; and as she'd walked in with the birthday boy Melissa had been automatically welcomed and, in some cases, embraced. Drinks were instantly placed into their hands, they'd both been pulled into the midst of the chatter and music filled house. As Michael made the rounds, hugging and chatting to all those who wished him a happy birthday, Melissa wasn't given an opportunity to feel at all out of place. People milled around her, talking to her and asking her about herself. Everyone was friendly and she was able to relax completely and enjoy the party.

A girl that Melissa hadn't noticed before gave her a warm smile, which she'd returned before continuing to refill her glass with cola from the bottle on the drink-covered table, not noticing when the girl's smile dropped a notch and a hard glint briefly twinkled in her eyes. Without being aware of it, those around her looked uneasy as the girl who had smiled so fondly at Melissa began to walk over.

Grant, who was Michael's oldest friend and one of the few people at the party who wasn't drinking, quickly moved next to her.

"You enjoying the party, Melissa?" he asked as he grabbed a can of cola and opened it.

Smiling sweetly and answering honestly, Melissa answered, "It's great. I can't remember when I last had such a good time!"

Before Grant could say whatever he had opened his mouth to say, the girl with the bleach-blonde hair had appeared at Melissa's side.

"You're Michael's girlfriend?"

She quickly quelled the guilt that began to churn as she heard that question. Melissa could now see the hard quality in the girl's alcohol-hazed light-brown eyes, the too-sweet smile that seemed to curdle as Melissa looked at it. "Yes."

Meaning to be obvious, the girl who could have actually looked pretty if it hadn't been for the thick covering of make-up, looked Melissa up and down. "You don't *look* like a nutcase." Her voice carried well and even people who were in the far edges of the room turned to look.

"What do you mean?" Melissa asked in a small voice.

Michael began to move towards the two girls, a look of apprehension on his face but made it only halfway before the girl's words brought him to a stop.

"You're prettier than I thought, too. You know, from the way Michael talked about you. But, really, you don't look quite the self-harming, suicidal freak I was expecting!"

Melissa felt the blood draining from her face and yet at the same time she could feel her cheeks burning. There were so many people standing there watching, staring as Melissa's secrets were spilled out of the drunken girl's lips. Although her eyes remained on the girl before her, Melissa was able to see Michael standing, watching, like the others. Why wasn't he coming to help her?!

Nobody else around her seemed capable of movement, nor did they seem able to look away. Yet, to their credit, they all looked almost distraught by the scene that was playing out before them.

"Michael told me *all* about it, you know." Before Melissa was able to move away, like a snake striking a mouse, the blonde had reached forwards and pushed the sleeves of Melissa's top up to the elbows, the pale, long scars on the underside of her arms clear to everyone around her.

The distress on Melissa's face forced Grant into action and, livid with himself for not having intervened sooner, he pushed the girl away from her, fury etched on his face. "Back off, Claire!"

Tears starting to break through her eyes, Melissa walked

through the crowd of people. None of them laughed or jeered at her, but their sympathetic glances and compassionate smiles made her feel worse than their mocking could have done. As they cleared a path for her to go outside, she made sure that she kept away from Michael. She wanted to be nowhere near the cowardly bastard.

As she left the room, walking out into the hallway and out through the front door, she heard an explosion of noise as people began to throw a tirade of abuse at the girl she now knew was called Claire.

The sky was clear, the stars bright above her, and she inhaled the cold winter air into her lungs, feeling it freeze her throat. She pushed her sleeves back down and wrapped her arms around herself, but the cold penetrated the flimsy protection.

She stiffened a few minutes later when a jacket was draped over her shoulders. The tears in her eyes were now down to the bitter cold rather than her immense shame, and she refused to allow herself to believe that she had to hide them.

"There's a part of me that wants to ask if you're okay," Grant said, the soft blue eyes gently searching her face. "But I think I know just how much a stupid question that would be."

Melissa regarded him for a second, seeing his kind expression below the short blonde hair that had been gelled up a little. This was Michael's best friend, so why was he out here with *her* and not inside where Michael still was? In fact, why was he out here at all, when it should be Michael standing there?

"Yeah," she said, her voice soft but still strong. "It is a bit of a stupid question." She managed to form a smile to show him that she wasn't offended. "But thanks for wondering."

He continued to look at her.

"But, I'm okay. It's just when she started saying that..." She broke off, and after a moment when more words wouldn't come, she walked down the car-filled drive to perch herself on the small brick wall that surrounded the garden.

Grant followed her over and leant casually against the wall next to where she sat, his hands stuffed deep into his jeans pockets. "Everyone in there knows that she was out of order, Melissa. There isn't one person in there who doesn't hate her right now."

"Thanks. I just don't know why I was the target."

Grant's mood rose a little. "Claire's just your standard party skank."

Melissa laughed; she couldn't help it, not with the amusement that had filled his voice when he'd said that. "A party skank?"

Encouraged, Grant smiled and looked at her. "Yeah. You know, goes to a party dressed as tartily as possible, make-up trowelled onto her face, makes sure that she gets as pissed as possible, and makes a play for anyone that might have her. She used to always make a play for Michael—"

Melissa had smiled for all of his speech until he mentioned Michael. She had a flash memory of the marks that had appeared on his chest after the Halloween party, and her smile fell.

"But now he's with you, so she's really pissed off. But she'll soon move onto someone else. That's something about the legendary Party Skank – someone else always comes along because they're such an easy lay."

Despite it all, a small twinkle formed in her eyes behind the sadness. "So, did *you* ever…?"

"Melissa!" Grant stood up straight, away from the wall so that he could look at her. He feigned offence, but his grin gave him away. "Even in my drinking days, I was never *that* drunk!"

She joined him in laughter and felt a touch of the hurt slide away. She glanced at the door, which Grant saw.

"Ready to go back in?"

She nodded and slipped off the wall. With Grant walking beside her, they went back into the house.

Although a number of people still glanced at her a little wearily, embarrassed smiles flittering across faces, most just waved friendlily if they caught her eye and then continued dancing or talking. Melissa began to feel okay until she noticed a couple in amongst the others that danced, and she knew that she didn't really belong there.

He didn't look thrilled but neither was he walking away as Claire moved in making what she obviously thought were sexy movements around him, her dress-sheathed body rubbing against his.

Grant touched Melissa's arm so that she turned to look at him. Combined concern for her and anger towards Michael were clear in his eyes. "Do you want me to take you home?"

Melissa nodded.

The journey back to Melissa's wasn't exactly uncomfortable, but it definitely wasn't easy. Grant seemed to want to say something, anything, to make her feel better, but there were no words that would be able to help. So as not to give him the slightest invitation to try to ease what was in her heart, Melissa stared resolutely out of the window, watching the streetlamps as the car moved past them, looking at the night that occupied the space in between.

When the car stopped outside her house, Grant made no attempt to step out of the car. With the engine still running, he turned to watch as Melissa slipped his coat from around her shoulders.

"He's an idiot, Melissa. But I do think he cares a great deal for you."

She looked deeply into his eyes, her lips moved into a sad smile. "Just not enough, I guess."

Without giving him a chance to respond, Melissa swung the door open and stepped out, leaving his jacket on the seat she had just vacated. Before she closed the door she leaned and said, "Thanks, Grant."

"No problem, Melissa. Take it easy, okay?"

She nodded and said goodbye, closing the car door firmly. It wasn't until she was in the house, the door locked behind her, that she heard Grant leave. He'd waited until she was safely inside before leaving.

The light bouncing off the blade and into her eyes was the first thing she saw when she woke up. The night had passed her by while she had relived the evening, and new pale daylight spilled into the room. Melissa raised her head from the table, wincing at the short shot of pain that travelled along her neck. She massaged it, moving her head from one side to the other, as she turned the light off, softly cursing herself for the fact that she had left it on all night.

The morning had dawned cloudless and a promise of a bright, if cold, day filled the air. Standing in the living room, looking out of the window into the dew-covered garden beyond, Melissa felt oddly calm. The pain of the night had vanished with the darkness, leaving her almost serenely content. She kicked off the shoes that had remained on her feet throughout the night, wiggling her toes to try to encourage a bit of feeling to work back into them, and still she looked out over the garden, still feeling the bizarre absence of pain and sadness. Even summoning back the memory of her scars being revealed to all those close enough to see, the humiliation that had consumed her then was nowhere in evidence.

The light was still soft as she ventured back downstairs after a hot shower, dressed in black jogging bottoms and a baggy blue T-shirt. She had dried her hair with her hair dryer, and it now bounced softly against her back as she walked to the kitchen.

Sitting on the back step, bare feet upon the cold surface of the paving slabs and a hot cup of coffee beside her, Melissa looked at the plants around her, seeing each individual drop of dew that covered everything, just waiting for the moment that the negativity would wash over her again. But as her drink cooled and the sky brightened, those feelings remained noticeably truant from inside her. It wasn't that she wished them to come back, she had no desire to put herself through more pain, especially if it was self-induced, but she wanted to be sure that they *weren't* going to return.

Melissa refilled her empty coffee cup twice, each time returning to her place on the step to continue her vigil over the garden, yet despair still did not attack her. Although not disappointed, she did feel a little miffed that she didn't feel worse. Resigning herself to her serenity, and rebuking herself for feeling so put out by the lack of sadness, she picked up her empty cup and went back into the kitchen, wiping her wet feet on the mat to rid the residue of moisture from their soles, and just in time to hear her mobile phone voice its shrill beep.

Seeing Michael's name underneath the announcement of the text still did not bring to her any anger or hurt, but that didn't mean that she wished to communicate with him in any way. Without reading the message she switched off her phone and put it on a shelf in her living room. She then unplugged her house phone in anticipation of its expected ring.

Glancing at the knife that was still on the table, Melissa put it back into its slot within the wooden knife block before returning to the living room to sit on the sofa. She tucked her legs up before her, crossing them in the same way she did when meditating, and ran her hands through her long, mousy brown hair, her soft but genuine laugh filling the room as she wondered just what the hell she was doing.

* * *

As expected, the phone beeped repeatedly after she turned it on, alerting her to the eleven text messages and three voice-mail messages that Michael had sent to her over the last two days. First she read the messages, reading the apologies without any real interest. Two of the three messages on the mobile's answer-phone were filled with Michael's apologetic, yet defensive, words; but the voice that filled the space between the two messages brought a feeling of soft warmth in the pit of her stomach.

Grant's voice was full of concern. "Melissa, it's Grant. I just wanted to check that you were doing okay. Give me a ring or drop me a text if you need anything."

Quickly she typed a text message to Grant, thanking him for worrying and assuring him that she was fine. Then, holding onto the clarity that had descended on her since the disaster of the party, she rang Michael.

He picked up between the first and second rings. "Melissa! Hi!"

"Hi, Michael."

"Look, Melissa, about the other nigh—"

"Michael, stop." She interrupted his flow of what, she supposed, would just have been a replay of all the messages. "Can you come round, please, so we can talk?"

"I can be there any time," he answered immediately.

"In about an hour?"

"Yeah, an hour. That's great!"

"See you then." As she closed her phone, she worried a little about the excitement that had been in his voice.

"So that's it? Just like that?!"

She sighed at the stubborn set of his jaw as he leant against the doorway between the kitchen and the living room, the empty cup held loosely as he looked at her.

"Not 'just like that', Michael. There's—"

"It feels 'just like that' to me!"

Melissa's eyes flickered to the cup held tightly. It was getting unnerving; he kept loosening his grip then tightening it again, the muscles in his arms flexing.

The temptation to lay the blame on his behaviour at the party, to dump all of the responsibility on to his shoulders, was almost too much; it would be so easy. But it wasn't right; no matter what he had done (or not done, by standing there and letting Claire humiliate her), he deserved the truth of it all.

She rose from the sofa and took a couple of steps towards him. "Michael, it's not just because of what happened the other night." Pausing, Melissa wished that she didn't always feel the need to be so honest. "I've been thinking about finishing things for a little while."

Michael's face lost that stubborn frame, engulfed by a mixture of shock, pain and anger. Then the first two expressions melted away, only anger remaining. "Well, that's just FUCKING FANTASTIC!"

Melissa cringed as the cup he held in his hand was projected forwards, the porcelain shattering against the wall behind the sofa.

As he looked at the place of its impact, his arm slowly lowering to his side, the fury vanished, leaving him looking injured. "God, Melissa. I'm so sorry. I didn't mean to do that. I'll get something to clean it up."

For a moment she just stood there, listening as he knocked her spare keys in his search for cleaning supplies. When she heard him opening cupboard doors she moved into the kitchen.

"I'll do it, Michael. I think you should just go."

He nodded, without arguing and strode quietly past her. A moment later the sound of the front door closing declared his exit.

Grabbing a bag to put the shards of the cup in and a cloth, dampening it slightly, she went back into the living room, having not noticed that the space on the kitchen counter that was normally filled by her spare keys was now empty.

Chapter Nine

It was going to take a little getting used to. Each time she passed the mirrors (or even if she happened to catch her reflection in the window), she would be shocked into a sudden stop, before laughing at her own surprise. It had been six days since she'd asked Michael to leave her alone and three since her visit to the hairdresser's, yet her new look still caused a butterfly feeling in her stomach, a pleasant tingling which only ever came to her when she achieved something good, even when it came on such a small scale.

She put down her hairbrush after brushing her hair for far too long, and looked in the mirror. The setting sun was shining through the window, highlighting one side of her hair, turning the brown strands into a fiery auburn. She moved her gaze to look deep into her own eyes, and saw the same fire burning there; and found herself momentarily caught. Leaning forwards, looking into the depths of those blazing eyes, noting all the specks and flecks that made up the green, she searched herself.

It had been a long time since she had last soul-gazed – too long! – but it felt like the right time, with the euphoria caused by the simple change of her now above-shoulder hair.

Her green eyes were still on fire, and as she stared deep she could feel her euphoria receding, to allow in the knowledge she was looking for. As she always did, she saw the underlining sadness, the constant that had been the foundation she had built on. But the sadness *was* only the foundation. What was shining through now was confidence and strength.

And it was that strength that moved her from the vanity table, moved her around the side of the bed; moved her to stand in front of her wardrobe. The weak voice in the back of her mind told her it was a mistake, but she easily dismissed it. After all, she had the strength to, had seen it herself.

She moved the box of poems out, and then pulled out the other box. Before doubt had time to find its way back in and as she sat back on her heels before it, Melissa lifted the lid.

An aura of perfume wafted out from the box, causing an ache so deep in her heart that tears welled in her eyes instantly. The flowery scent, so unlike anything she'd ever used herself, was so strong, the image it brought to her so clear.

Hands shaking wildly, Melissa rummaged quickly through the papers, photographs and other bits and pieces that filled the box, until her skin touched the soft cotton. Eyes closed, she brought it out and held it to her face, feeling the fibres and inhaling the scent. With her eyes closed, she looked at Lauren, saw the braces that ran across her top teeth; the hair, just that one shade lighter than Melissa's, hanging in a plait down her back. She saw her laughing as she played; crying on the rare occasion when that had resulted in a tumble. Breathing in the scent of her little sister's perfume, pushing back the tears as a mass of memories exploded in her mind, she smiled softly before placing the folded garment back into its place at the bottom of the box, next to the small soft purple teddy bear that was infused with the fragrance.

Moving things around, taking out photographs she'd kept hidden for years, placing them beside her, she also brought out a white envelope. She looked at the shaky script, the scrawling of a person in dire need of a fix of their particular poison, and looked at the top edge that had been ripped open all those years ago. Feeling it was this that she had meant to retrieve from the box of her past, she closed it back up and put both of the cardboard containers back in their proper places.

Pagan folk music played softly from the speakers, the living room filled with the sound of flutes and bodhrans. The sun lit the room, bouncing off the walls with its rich but fading light as she set the photos and letter on the arm of the sofa before walking into the kitchen. As she was not a regular drinker, her wine glasses were in a top cupboard on a high shelf. Instead of using a dining chair to stand on as she would normally do, she turned so that she was facing away from the cupboard and placing her hands flat on the counter surface she boosted herself up. Sitting with her legs dangling, feet swinging a little and feeling like a child, she reached behind herself, opened the door and stretched her arm out so she could grab a glass. She set it down and dropped back down to the floor.

The bottle of rosé wine was cold as she took it from the fridge and poured herself a glass, tilting the glass so that the liquid glided down the inside of the long curved surface. Leaving the bottle on the kitchen counter, moisture beginning to pool at the bottom of the outside of the bottle, she took her drink to the coffee table next to her sofa. She was about to sit down but stopped, and looked down at her clothes.

Smiling, she went back to her bedroom, returning only when she had changed out of her confining jeans. She lay along the sofa in loose-fitting jogging bottoms and equally loose T-shirt, half-sitting with her back resting in the corner against the arm of the seat, and took a sip of her wine.

It was a wonderful combination, enhancing the positive feelings that had risen in her: the setting sun, turning the room into a furnace of rich light, the comfort as she relaxed on the soft-seated sofa, the flowery taste of the wine on her tongue, and the gentle music surrounding her. The thought that she had nearly killed herself out of pain and despair had never seemed so far away, the scars had never seemed so faded. Even the pain that she was about to put herself through seemed sweet.

She sipped her wine occasionally as she looked through the photographs. There were none of her father, no record of his existence in the small group of pictures, and very few of her mother. Many of the photos contained Melissa and Lauren together; but most were just of Lauren. Lauren as a baby; Lauren walking her first few steps; her first day of school, looking so cute in her school uniform – and one with them together, both in uniform, the six years that had separated them only allowing them in the same school for a single year; photos showing each birthday party through the years; Lauren laughing; Lauren smiling mischievously at the camera lens and whoever had been behind it at the time. Lauren at eight years old, the oldest she would ever reach. Just eight.

Making a promise to herself to buy some picture frames so that her sister's image could be displayed as it should be, promising that the pictures were out of that box for good, she left them to one side and picked up the letter.

The envelope had been folded many times and creases ran along it in all directions, almost like the lines on the palm of a hand, or like the scars of a person struggling for control. Still drinking her wine, her head starting to swim pleasantly as the alcohol worked its way through her system, Melissa ran her index finger over her name and the address that had been printed on the front. The house that the letter had been sent to. The first of two foster homes that she had lived in, had been lovely, the family who had taken her in had also been lovely; but it had never been her home. But the smiles came easily as she thought of those kind people, the two who had tried to be parents to her and the girl who had tried to be a sister. The second couple she had lived with had been nice, too; a couple with no children of their own, whose only sin had been the inability to understand the distance that she'd needed after all she had been through. They just hadn't known how to interact with someone like her.

The large writing that covered the single sheet of paper, both sides, was as shaky as that on the envelope and grew worse closer to the end.

My darling daughter,

I'm shaking as I write this to you, Melissa, not only out of emotion, but out of withdrawal. I haven't had a drink in six days – SIX WHOLE

DAYS without a single drop! I know that it doesn't seem much (although it seems like an eternity to me already) but it's a start. I'm going to do it, this time, Mellie. I really am!

The social worker told me that you're doing well. She said that you've settled in with the Atkinsons and that you've started your new school. I hope that you're OK, that things are going really well, and that you're happy. It won't be forever, Melissa. I swear to you, it won't be forever. I just need to get the drinking under control first – they have to be sure that I won't relapse again. They have to make sure that it's safe you to come home to me. That I can look after myself again so that I'm able to look after you properly.

And I'm doing it for you, Mellie. I can never forgive myself for being so blind.

Melissa seethed slightly, as she always had when reading that line, and wished that her mother was with her in person, so that she could tell her that the truth that she had never been *blind*: instead, the woman whose job it was to protect her children had *chosen* not to see, had *chosen* to look away, to bury herself in the bottom of a bottle. And had then, with a single phone call, ended her youngest daughter's life. But the denial of her own responsibility had been clear in that letter, even all those years ago.

She drained her glass and read on, reading words already read hundreds of times.

And I'm doing it for you, Mellie. I can never forgive myself for being so blind, for allowing all of those terrible things to happen. I can never forgive myself for not being able to save Lauren. But I also know that I can't change things, I can't bring Lauren back to us. All I can do is what I'm doing. All I can do is sort myself out so that I can make things better for you, my little girl. You're the reason I'll keep trying! You're the reason I'm going to make it!

It's not like last time. I'm really working hard. I'm going to the meetings every day, and I speak to the counsellor every day, and I phone him when I want to drink really badly. It isn't easy, most of the time it's SO HARD! But I'll do it!

I miss you, Melissa, and I love you more than I can ever tell you.

Hugs and kisses, my Mellie.

Mum

xxxxxxx

Melissa folded the letter up and put it back into the envelope. She went into the kitchen and poured herself another drink, knowing that it would have to be her last one – she really couldn't handle too much alcohol in one go. She was one of the few people that she'd ever known that knew her limit and never went beyond it. The bottle went back in the fridge and she stood looking out of the kitchen window.

The sun had descended closer to the horizon, but the sky was still submerged in dark reds and oranges, twilight still a little time away. Quickly, she bundled herself up in her winter coat and braved the early-December evening air, sitting on the step and gazing out into the garden.

Melissa sat, drinking her wine, until she greeted the dark night, the stars shining brightly in the depth of the sky.

She sat on the floor in front of the TV, refusing to take her eyes off the screen but not seeing what images played there. She wanted to take it back. She wanted to go back to the teacher, the lovely woman who had taught her English; the lovely, caring woman who had made it so easy for Melissa to let go of the terrible secret. She wanted to go back to the woman she had confided in before running out of the classroom in tears, and tell her that it wasn't true, tell her that the awful secret she had carried for so long had just been a lie. Melissa knew that a lot of people her age often lied to get attention; surely they would believe her if she told them that it was a lie!

What stopped her, what kept her sitting still on the floor with her eyes glued to the television screen, was Lauren. Her little sister, six years younger than her big sister, eight to Melissa's incredible age of fourteen. God knew that Lauren could drive Melissa up the wall sometimes! Her over-energetic moods, her little pranks, and the constant arguments between the two of them (where Lauren would call her 'weirdo', and Melissa would call her 'train-track' due to the braces she had fixed to her teeth). But she was Lauren's big sister, and since their mother wouldn't protect them, it was her job to look out for the baby of the family instead. She knew that she was already too late to stop it from happening, had heard Lauren crying last night; but she could at least make sure it wouldn't happen again!

Her head snapped sharply to the right, to the doorway between the living room and the hallway, as several loud knocks hit the front door. And now it was the doorway that Melissa couldn't take her eyes from, staring at the empty space while her stomach turned uneasily, while her hands grew clammy. She watched as her mother walked casually past the door, moving from the kitchen towards the front door, her body swaying in the already-drunk swagger that was the norm – even at the tender time of half past four in the afternoon.

As the sound of her mother fumbling to find some purchase on the door handle came floating to her ears, Melissa bolted to the window. Two new cars were parked on the drive where usually only her father's car sat. One of them was just a white car, nothing exceptional or noticeable about it. The other was very *noticeable. A police car was parked behind the other, blocking it in. Out of the corner of her eye, with the sound of men and women talking to her drunk mother at the threshold of the house, Melissa could see a few of her neighbours looking curiously at the appearance of the police officers.*

Voices were growing louder as they drew closer and, slowly, she looked around to see two women – one wearing a light-coloured trouser suit, and the other in jeans and a blouse – walking into the room. Behind them, two police officers, both male, followed. And then her mum walked in.

Guilt exploded within Melissa's heart as she saw the anger in her mum's eyes. Beneath the alcohol-induced haze that anger shot out, aimed at the girl whose crime it had been to try and protect her little sister from having to live through the same hell that she'd had to survive.

"Melissa," one of the women, the one in the jeans with the soft curls in her light brown hair, said as they walked closer to her. "My name's Christine. We want to have a little chat, Melissa, okay? About what you said to your teacher?"

"Excuse me a moment."

As her mother began to walk out of the room, one of the police officers turned. "Mrs Adams, we really need you to stay here."

He reached out to gently take hold of her arm, his fingers no more than brushing the material of her jumper, when she whirled around. Viciously, she pushed him back, forcing him to fall against his colleague, before she ran out of the room. The stunned men quickly regained their composure and chased her out of the room.

A door slammed closed – which Melissa recognised as the door to the downstairs toilet – before the police officers started hammering on the wooden partition, shouting for her to open it. Christine, who would become the social worker that Melissa would have the most contact with, drew closer and put an arm around the fourteen-year-old's quivering shoulders.

Melissa listened as one of the police officers spoke over his radio, telling the person on the other end of the airwaves that Samantha Adams had locked herself into a room and, using a mobile phone, had alerted Patrick Adams to the situation. He told the person on the other end of the radio that Patrick Adams was driving his own car, and that he was currently alone with the youngest daughter, Lauren Adams. Melissa listened as the police officer instructed a person she would never meet to start a search.

She then heard the door open and, with a stranger's arm around her, heard her mother being placed under arrest. And, with a stranger's arm around her, Melissa thought about Lauren, about her little sister, who was alone with their father.

She knew that she was awake straight away, that the memory-dream had ended with her sleep, and that she was safe in her bed, in her own house. That she was no longer fourteen, but twenty-three, and that those things had happened a long time ago.

She also knew that she felt the desire to harm, had awoken with the craving already filtering through her body. It tingled in her, an itch that she longed to give in to. She indulged in the torture of her craving for a while, staring at the ceiling, feeling the slight thumping in her head and the fuzzy feeling on the surface of her tongue, signalling that she really should have had more water after her wine the night before.

Five minutes later she sat on the sofa, waiting for the ibuprofen tablets she'd taken to kick in and begin working. The television was on, the sound low, a talk show host pretentiously introducing a guest. Randomly, she chose a DVD from her small DVD case and put it on – not caring in the least what it was, only caring that the daytime programme was no longer the thing that was killing the silence. When it was playing, she settled back on to her sofa and picked up the scissors she'd brought down with her. Gently she ran the ball of her thumb over one of the open blades. Sluggishly, she moved the blade to hover over her left arm.

Then she simply closed them and put them back on the table beside her, picking up her glass of water, sipping it. Without focus, she stared at the television, turning occasionally to glance at the would-be cutting equipment. Although thinking about that memory, having relived it in her sleep, should have triggered her to cut, her mind almost demanding it, Melissa realised that she didn't really *want* to. What she had mistaken for the compulsion to hurt herself had merely been her mind's habitual reaction to thinking about something from her past; it was her mind saying, 'That's what you normally do in this situation, so that's what you *should* do now!'

Halfway through the film that played without any of it penetrating her thoughts, she switched it off. She took the scissors back to the bathroom and put them away.

* * *

Andrew finished writing in her file, clicked off his pen and sat back in his chair, pushing his glasses up to their proper place high on the bridge of his nose.

There were so many things she was doing, so many positive steps that she was taking to improve her life: Finishing with her boyfriend to end the continual knocks to her self-confidence; the new hairstyle; using the internet to start looking for work; pushing herself to bring up the past, and recognising when the habit of self-harm tried to push in. She really was doing so well.

Yet there was something. Something that Andrew, with all his training in counselling and psychology, could pin down to nothing except gut instinct. There was something that just wasn't right, and he felt a tremble of fear at the base of his spine for Melissa.

Chapter Ten

She couldn't find them! She always left them in her kitchen, but although she had turned the room inside out, she was unable to see even a glimpse of the bunch of keys. She'd quickly scanned her living room to see if she might have put them down somewhere there, but there was just no sign of them. It just wasn't like her to leave them elsewhere. She couldn't even remember the last time she'd seen them. Not that it mattered, not really. They were bound to turn up sometime and she didn't need them straight away. They were just the spare keys and she still had her main ones. She knew that, deep down, it was just a delaying tactic she was using. She was really dreading going.

Her mood lifted slightly when she walked into the living room. The decorations infused the room with happiness. The silver and red tinsel entwined with the natural streams of ivy, pinecones and mistletoe. Cinnamon sticks and bayberries were dotted throughout, filling the room with their combined scents. Her mood dipped again as she saw the gift sitting on the dining table. With her eyes closed she inhaled deeply, filling her nose with the aromas around her, pulling as much peace into herself as she could. Then she grabbed the present and her car keys, and left the house.

The small one bedroom flat that her mother lived in was on the other side of town, and driving there Melissa passed houses that had been engulfed by the festive season and were draped in Christmas decorations. Everything from subtle outside lights to those with huge illuminated Santas, giant inflatable snowmen, and enough lights that would put Vegas to shame. As tacky as some of it was, it took Melissa back to those few golden moments of the Christmases of her childhood. Even the large block of flats sent out waves of pulsating lights into the darkening day as she arrived.

She pulled into the parking bay that was reserved for her mother's flat and took the small wrapped package from the passenger seat footwell. Using the key that her mother had given her shortly after moving in to the small block, Melissa opened the lobby doors, letting them slip securely closed behind her, and ascended the concrete stairs. The lifts in the building had never had the pleasure of her company – her claustrophobia and nervousness of being enclosed (and likely with people she wouldn't know) forced her to avoid the moving metal boxes.

After knocking a couple of times and getting no answer, with her other key she let herself into her mother's flat. The heat inside impacted on her the second she opened the door. A glance at the thermostat showed her it was set to twenty-six degrees.

"Mum?" she called out softly while removing the layers of coats, scarf and jumper that had been necessary for braving the mid-December evening but were now redundant. "Mum?!" She shouted again as she dropped them all in a pile on top of the shoe rack.

There was still no response from her mother but she could hear the television playing loudly in the main room, so headed there.

No decorations filled the room, no tinsel, no lights and no tree, but Melissa still felt like smiling a little. The place was cleaner then she'd expected it to be; it appeared that her mother had re-learnt some of her housekeeping skills since Melissa's last visit, which was almost a year ago. But her new-found cleanliness couldn't mask the underlining smell of alcohol.

Rounding the corner, she stared at the zombie-like form of Samantha Adams lounging on the tatty three-seat sofa, a drink in hand, eyes on the TV. Melissa stood there, so far unnoticed, and reprimanded herself for not coming to the flat sooner; she knew that, when she had to visit, it was always better to see her mother in the morning, before the total of drinks consumed began to rise too high. But her own reluctance to come here and pushed aside her good sense.

"Mum," she said again, and this time the woman's head turned.

"Hi, Mellie." Although her voice was slurred, it wasn't as bad as it normally would be at this time of the evening, nor were her brown eyes as bloodshot as she was accustomed to seeing them. Melissa felt something close to pride as she looked at her mum; she had a feeling that the woman before her, looking much older than her actual years, had limited her drinks for Melissa's visit.

"It's warm in here." She crossed the small room to sit on the hard backed chair opposite.

"You know I don't like the cold." She looked at her daughter curiously, brow creased in concentration as she tried to realise what was different. It took her a little while, but she got there. "You've had your hair cut."

"Fancied a change. It's been the same length most of my life, so I decided to do something totally different."

"It suits you," she said, almost dismissively, as she turned her attention back to the TV while she gulped down some of the whiskey from her large glass.

Melissa looked through the doorway to the kitchen, and was surprised to see that it, too, looked clean. "The place looks good, Mum."

A raspy laugh followed that and Melissa looked back at her mum to see her smiling.

"You mean it looks tidy. I've started cleaning every day again. First thing in a morning, before too many of these –" she lifted her glass up, almost in a toast – "have magically disappeared." She laughed again before growing a little more serious. She looked at the floor, then back at her daughter. "You changed your phone number."

Melissa wondered if all mothers had the power to induce guilt in their children so easily, or if it was just her own mother who owned that particular skill. "I needed some space; some time to concentrate on me, so I can figure out some stuff."

Samantha nodded and added another swallow of her drink to whatever she'd already had, the momentarily wounded look slipping from her features.

"I brought you something." Melissa took the gift over to her mum before returning to the chair – she did this in the shortest time she could: she didn't like being too close to her mum.

"Thanks, Mellie." She looked almost sober as she studied the sparkly paper the book of poetry was wrapped in. Any appearance of sobriety faded, though, as she struggled to gain her feet. "I have something for you, too."

Melissa watched as her mum left the living room to venture into the bedroom, with the all-too-familiar swaying gait. She covered her mouth with her hand and stared at the TV, struggling to keep control. It was hard! Just being here was *so hard!* Not only was the smell of the booze starting to hurt her head, seeing her mother just hurt every inch of her. She waited for what seemed a very long time, in the too-hot room with the loud television as company, for her mum to come back.

Still struggling to find her balance as she moved, Samantha walked over to Melissa and held out a large box.

Even before she stretched her hand out in front of her, Melissa knew what the large present was; it was the same things she'd received from her mother for the last five years. But, despite the lack of imagination, the large box of chocolates had been carefully and perfectly wrapped, and she was able to thank her mother genuinely for the gift.

Looking pleased, Samantha stopped on her way to the sofa. She looked frustrated at herself. "I haven't even offered you a drink. Sorry, Mellie."

"That's okay, Mum."

"Did you want something? I've got whiskey, vodka. I think I've got a bottle of wine…"

"No, thanks. I'm driving."

"Coffee?"

"Coffee would be great." As her mother started to move sluggishly towards the kitchen, Melissa quickly met her and put a hand on her arm. She removed it immediately, as if an electric shock had gone through her. "I'll make it, Mum."

Waiting for the kettle to finish boiling, she marvelled at the complexity of her feelings towards her mother. She hated what her mum had allowed to happen in the past; hated what the woman had become. Yet still she felt the childlike need for approval, or acceptance, or closeness – or whatever it was that she felt she was missing. It was always so much easier for her to simplify her emotions when her mother was totally drunk and acting in any way except the way she should. When she was trying, it only confused things.

Melissa managed to stay for an hour, timed by the digital clock on her mother's DVD player. Although a little general conversation passed between the two women, most of the time was filled with only the sound of the TV as it showed one of the reality programmes that was another of her mother's addictions.

After putting her cup on the counter next to the sink, Melissa stood by the chair she'd been sitting in and picked up the gift she'd received. She once again looked, unnoticed, at the woman who stared at the television. "Mum. I'm going to have to go now."

Samantha pulled her gaze from the people on screen as they performed the ridiculous task that had been set for them, and looked at her daughter. "Okay, Mellie." She paused, looked as if she was going to attempt to stand, then decided against it. "Have a good Christmas."

"You too, Mum. Merry Christmas."

There were no hugs, no kisses exchanged. Melissa simply walked from the room, gathered her things from on top of the shoe rack and left the flat. Knowing that her mother wouldn't think to do it, Melissa locked the door behind her. Samantha

Adams just turned back to the TV and continued to drink herself into oblivion.

* * *

Friday the twenty-first of December was brought in by the sound of thunder and the heavy downpour of rain and hail. Muddy puddles appeared everywhere, springing up rapidly as the rain fell too quickly for the almost frozen ground to absorb. The sound as it hit the car in Melissa's drive and the roof of the house was deafening, obliterated only by the occasional loud crash of thunder and lightning flashes. Melissa slept through the first few hours of the storm, waking a few minutes past five when a particularly violent crack of lightning struck close by.

Her ears filled with the echoing noise, Melissa looked, wide-eyed, into the thick darkness around her, momentarily disorientated. There were no traces in her mind of the dream she had had while asleep, no clue as to where she had spent her dream-time, but her disorientation made her believe it was far from where she now was. Bit by bit, the sense of uncertainty drifted away to be replaced by an innocent wonder.

"It's Yule."

The whisper seemed to hang in the air, filling the room with a simple and undeniable joy and happiness. She felt like skipping and jumping out of the room! Instead, she lay where she was, smiling in the darkness, listening to the hammering of the rain. Other than the gift from her mother, there were no presents to open like there had been on the Christmas mornings that she had shared with her family. But that same excitement remained, and returned in entirety each Yule.

In the dark, she left her room and walked the familiar route down the stairs and to her living room. Without being able to see, she trekked into the room with its enveloping smells and to the mantelpiece. She easily found the long arched candleholder that she had set up the night before, along with the small lighter. On each end of the candleholder was a tall, dining candle, one red and one green. The one that crowned the apex of the arch was pure white.

With the lighter, she lit first the green candle and then moved to the left and lit the red, the light softly illuminating her features, and she felt the warmth of the flames on her face. She looked at the white candle in the centre and held the lighter ready. As she spoke her whispering breath caused the already lit candles to flicker slightly.

"For the rebirth of the Lord of the Forest. For the promise of the Light and Life to come. For the Spring that promises life. For the Wheel that turns ever onwards, leading me along my Path. Blessed Be."

Speaking the last words, a glowing stillness over her mind, she lit the last candle. She could see the three symbols on each of the candles that had been engraved with a pin the night before, seeming almost to dance in the flame light: the symbol of the Goddess, a circle flanked by two crescents, representing the three phases of the Moon; the symbol of the God, a circle crowned by a crescent, representing the Forest King's horns; and a circle quartered, the continuous Wheel with four spokes, representing the Solstices and Equinoxes.

With only the light from the three candles in the living room, Melissa moved around her shadowy kitchen and made herself a cup of tea without adding milk. She dropped a cinnamon stick into the tannin water, leaving it for a minute. As she made her way to her sofa, she lifted the cup and inhaled, revelling in the aroma. She sat, with the candles before her and the steady drumming of the rain outside the windows, and drank her cinnamon tea.

The rain continued all day, although the electricity-charged storm moved on around midday. The day never brightened, the thick dark clouds refused to allow any of the cold winter sunlight through. But Melissa didn't mind; in fact, she loved the sense that twilight had consumed the whole daylight hours, and that the three candles she had lit as soon as she'd risen were all that lit the world she was in.

The morning was spent in that softly-lit room, the curtains closed as she sat in her pyjamas watching the flames dance gently in the unperceivable draughts caught them, cinnamon-spiced tea giving way to coffee as the hours progressed, just drinking in the peace that she had woken with. When the sound of the rain had abated slightly, Melissa conceded and, after opening her curtains (which only lifted the darkness inside the room a fraction), she went upstairs and ran a shower.

An hour later, her hair still slightly damp, Melissa lifted a tray of chocolate chip and almond cookies from the oven. An array of different aromas saturated the kitchen, overpowering the Yuletide scents from the living room. The baked biscuits added their own recognisable contributions, but it was the aroma of the mulled apple cider simmering on the hob that now began to dominate the rest of the delicious scents. Even as she lifted the biscuits from the baking tray to the cooling rack, she could pick out the different ingredients from the drink; the clove-studded oranges, the cinnamon, and the nutmeg that all added to the alcohol-free cider's taste.

After putting the baking tray back into the oven to cool until she was ready to wash it, Melissa took out her teapot. There was no way she could not smile as she poured the amber liquid into the pot; it wasn't its originally intended use, but it was perfect for keeping the cider warm.

She wrapped her hands around the cup, almost as if she were trying to warm them, and she sat on the sofa with her legs up, a small plate with a number of cookies sitting stacked in the centre resting on the table beside her. Normally she would eat her warm cider and cookies outside, wrapped up tightly against the bitter cold, the heat from her food and drink meaning more because of the cold. But the ground was too wet for that, so—

She almost choked on the mouthful of cookie crumbs as she started laughing. She looked out through the window at the darkness outside and at the patterns that the rain was making on the glass panes. It was too wet for her to sit outside to enjoy her festival snack, and it was *definitely* too wet for her to walk to the bottom of the garden. The large chimenea at the far end of the lawn, standing on a small circle of stone, was the ideal place for her to safely burn the Yule log that had been put aside earlier in the year. But a torrent of rain stood between her and it. True, there was always the chance it could stop raining; she only ever burnt the log just before midnight, so there was still time for the rain to play out. But there was a chance that it wouldn't.

"Mmm," she said to herself gently after she had washed down the hazardous crumbs with a sip of her drink. "Guess I'll have to think of something else, just in case."

She had washed and put away the cutlery and plates, the kitchen once again clean and tidy. She had sliced up the leftover pork from her dinner, left it to cool and then put in the fridge, ready to be eaten for lunch tomorrow. A fresh batch of mulled cider, this time complete with alcohol, simmered gently on the stove, and spices again filled the air. Darkness had swallowed the muted light whole, and the three candles, now only half an inch left of each, had ceased to be enough. The light from the spotlights on the kitchen ceiling streamed through into the living room.

Melissa stood, looking past her own dark reflection, and through to the rain that still hammered the ground. The wind had changed direction, no longer forcing the water against the living room windows but driving it away. The log that she had set aside was on the windowsill next to a clear glass ashtray, but as it neared midnight it seemed that its purpose would not be completely fulfilled tonight.

While her dinner had cooked, Melissa had searched through her spare room. Eventually she had found a small light-brown cloth wrap, tied with its own fastenings. She opened it now, laying out the display of small woodcarving tools. It had been years since the last time she'd even opened them; the last time she had actually put them to use she had been in her early teens, and they hadn't been overly sharp then. Now they were almost blunt, but they would still do what she needed them to.

Choosing one with the widest furrows, she used the palm of her hand to push the handle down, carving out a thick sliver, which she dropped into the ashtray.

Ignoring the slight throbbing in her palm from the pressure exerted by pushing the chisel through the wood, she fetched a box of long matchsticks from the drawer furthest from the cooker. Despite how dry the wood was, it still took longer than she expected for it to ignite; the flame had reached halfway down the matchstick and she was beginning to feel the heat on her fingertips. Once she saw flames licking the edges of the wood, she dropped the match alongside it without extinguishing it and watched as the two flames joined together.

The cider was ready and with a cup in her hand, she turned off the gas underneath the pan and switched the kitchen lights off. She pulled a dining chair to the window, again in the dark except for the candles and the large burning chip of wood, and sat down. There, she stared out at the rain-infused dark, thinking of nothing – just letting the energy of the night fill her.

* * *

"What are you doing here?"

In a total contrast to the weather that had filled Yule, the sky of the twenty-third was clear of clouds but packed full of sparkling stars, brighter and stronger than she'd seen them in a long while. It was just another thing about winter that Melissa loved. But her appreciation of the clear, if bitterly cold, night was lost.

Michael looked nervous and completely unsure of himself as he stood in her doorway. He seemed completely different to the self-assured person she had first met in the tattooist's studio. "I, er…I wanted to drop this off to you." He picked up the large brown paper-wrapped parcel that was leaning against his right leg.

"What is it?" Looking at the dimensions, Melissa knew what it had to be, but that wasn't exactly what she meant.

"A Yule present." Seeing her cautious look, he held his free hand out to her. "I bought it before we split up, and I'd still really like you to have it. Though I will understand if you don't want to."

Still feeling unsure, she nevertheless opened the door wider and moved aside so that he could walk in. "Would you like a drink?"

"Yeah, that would be good." He followed as she walked through to the kitchen, leaving the parcel in the living room, against the side of the sofa.

Melissa made two cups of coffee and gave one to Michael. As she sipped her own, she looked at him. The silence between them was filled with awkwardness, filled with polite conversations that had no place to start.

Eventually, after many moments of looking at each other and many more moments of avoiding the other's eyes, Michael broke the stale quiet. "Are you going to open it?"

The directness of his question – especially given the silence they had occupied – was tempered by the obvious concern of his tone, and Melissa smiled. "I'm not sure."

"Well, the purpose of a present is for it to be received properly." Michael said as he placed his cup on the side next to the kettle. "But you can't fully receive something if you don't know what it is." He took Melissa's cup from her and placed it next to his own.

"I suppose that's true." Melissa still smiled, but the hammering of her heart sped up a little as he took one of her hands and led her back into the living room.

Guilt wafted through her as she held the parcel and sat on the sofa with it on the floor before her, her finger touching an edge of the paper where she would be able to begin removing it. "I didn't get you anything, Michael, I'm sorry."

He shook his head. "I wasn't expecting you to have."

Regardless of the circumstances, she would never be able to deny that opening the gift brought her a lot of pleasure. Beneath the brown wrapping, the wooden picture frame held the painting securely, and Melissa took her time revealing it. Only when she had removed the last part of the paper, taken out of the way quickly by her guest, did she turn it to face her.

Her breath caught in her chest, and for a moment breathing was the last thing on her mind. Ultimately, her body remembered what function it was supposed to be performing and resumed its task; but Melissa was unaware. Her eyes, her mind and her heart were all focussed on the print that was held so perfectly within the dark mouldered confines. She already knew the picture, had lovingly looked upon it many times; but the image captured in books and on the internet were nothing. *This* was real, the scene vibrant, each line and dash of colour screaming out for her attention.

"I know it's not the best quality there is," Michael said as he watched her studying it intensely, her eyes moving almost randomly over the picture,

"No. It's perfect." She looked up, and the moisture in her eyes was clear. "But I'm not sure that I can accept it, Michael."

He grinned impishly. "Well, you kind of need to. You see, I *accidentally* threw away the receipt, so I can't return it. And it's not really my kind of thing. So, the only other option would be to give it away, and I wouldn't want to see it go to someone who wouldn't really appreciate it."

Standing up, she stood her newly acquired print of Salvador Dali's *Metamorphosis of Narcissus* back against the sofa. She put her arms around Michael's neck and pulled him close, hugging him tight. "Thank you," she whispered in his ear, the warmth of his arms travelling through her thin jumper as they went around her waist. "It's the most thoughtful present I've ever been given."

He moved his head as he hugged her back, his breath hot on her neck. Her eyes closed in pleasure as one of his arms pulled her waist closer to his body and the other hand travelled up her back, crushing her upper body to him as well.

In the aftermath of the break-up, she had forced out how good it felt to have someone holding her so tight and so close; feeling the warmth of him against her, his heart beating fast beneath his clothes. His lips moved across the sensitive skin of her neck, sending shots of tingling electricity through her whole body, kissing over her chin and gently touching her lips. She felt herself responding, her own lips parting, her fingers moving through the hair at the base of his neck. She pushed away the doubts that started to whisper deep in her mind. All she wanted was to continue kissing him, losing herself in the familiar closeness of him, the smell of him, the taste of him.

Breathless, he moved away a little, still keeping her close but far enough away for him to look into her green eyes, looking almost sad despite the heat in his flushed face. "Melissa, is there any way that you would ever give me another chance?"

Those whispered clamourings in her thoughts tried to claw their way to her attention again, but she managed to hush them with the longing in his eyes, the comforting warmth of his embrace. And the incredible thoughtful gift. It wasn't that he'd bought her something expensive (which she knew it must have been; she'd looked into buying herself a print in the past). The cost of the gift meant nothing to her. It was the thought that he'd put into it, to get her something that would mean so much to her.

"I think I'd like to give it another try."

Smiling cautiously, his eyebrows raised, he searched her eyes questioningly. When she nodded, he swept her up into his arms, kissing her more passionately than she'd ever experienced.

Over an hour later – Michael in only his jeans and Melissa in only a T-shirt – they ventured back downstairs. Michael's hair stuck up in places where Melissa had run her fingers through, and she smiled as she sat on the sofa and watched him walk into the kitchen. He had insisted that she sit and relax while he made them both fresh drinks.

Feeling serene, she rested her head back and closed her eyes, listening as he moved around the kitchen while the kettle began to heat the water. She heard the fridge door open and then close, and then heard as he dropped the milk bottle lid onto the tiled floor.

"Damn it," came the whisper from the kitchen. There was a pause, then he called through. "Melissa? Why is there a set of keys under the fridge?"

Her eyes opened and she raised her head to see Michael walking into the living room, the previously missing bunch of keys over one finger.

"They're my spare keys!" she said in surprise, almost bounding up off the sofa, the hem of her T-shirt rising a little as she got up. "I lost them a while ago. Couldn't find them anywhere."

"They were under the fridge. I dropped the top off the milk and it rolled underneath. When I went to get it, I saw these."

She took the set of three keys from him, surprised at the lack of dust on them given where they had been. "I thought I'd looked under the fridge and freezer."

"Guess not," he said, shrugging slightly and moving back to the kitchen.

Still looking at the keys in her hand, she felt puzzled. "No. I guess not."

* * *

Huddled up tight in the thick coat, the scarf wound tight around her throat to stop the Christmas Day cold attacking it, Melissa looked down at the gravestones. Her hands were hiding inside suede gloves, the insides doing more than just keeping out the cold; the soft linings were keeping her fingers nice and warm, which she needed so that she could hold the white rose without her fingers freezing. She crouched and gently placed the flower on the frosty ground at the base of the granite headstone. She looked at the etching that was now at eye level, at her sister's name that had been carved deeply into the stone. Her gloved fingers traced first over her name, and then over the teddy bear that had also been carved underneath.

As she stood, she glanced briefly at the stone next to Lauren's. The dates of birth were separated by almost thirty-three years, but their dates of death were painfully identical.

Melissa hated, even after all of these years, that her mother had allowed them to be buried side by side, that she hadn't insisted that the man who lay in the ground hadn't been cremated. She didn't want the familiar anger to build up, didn't want her sister's grave to be a place of anything but somewhere for her to show her love for the girl so cruelly taken, a place of sad reflection. But she could feel the hatred resuming its heated race through her veins.

There had been no need for her to be standing in a churchyard, having just laid a rose on the place where her eight-year-old sister had been laid to rest; no need for *any* of it! Her mother could have prevented it, *should* have prevented it. All of the pain and humiliation she and her sister had suffered at the hands of their father, and the agony of her sister's murder by those same hands. If her mother had just faced up to what had been happening on the other side of her bottles of alcohol. If her mother had just never made that last phone call to him.

Her eyelids dropped, taking her into a semi-darkness on the bright day, and she breathed slowly. Focussing on her breathing, on forcing away the thoughts of her parents, she filled her lungs with the icy cold air. When she opened them again, seeing the cloud of fog that was in front of her as she breathed out, she fixed her eyes on her sister's name.

Anger had gone, left with the warm air she had expelled from her mouth, leaving her with a soft ache. She smiled sadly, touched the top of her sister's headstone, and began to walk out of the graveyard, her feet crunching the frosty grass as she left.

Chapter Eleven

Furiously they moved above the covers, bodies drenched with sweat as they writhed against each other, Melissa's legs wrapped fast around him, Michael's hands pinning hers to the bed. Scratch marks covered his back, some of the wounds moving through his tattoo, echoing the scratches on Melissa's back. Her groans matched his as he reached deep inside her, both of them feeling the intensity building up, the heat increasing. She squeezed his hands and he returned the pressure, the world fading except for the two of them. They climaxed within seconds of each other, both screaming out into the night-filled room.

He continued to lay on top of her and inside her, hands still holding hers against the bed, and kissed her softly on the lips. They rearranged themselves, pulling the covers over their bodies, so that she was lying beside him with her head resting on his chest, her arm resting on his stomach, and her fingers caressing over the fine hairs on his torso. His arm, which she lay on, wound around her back, holding her close.

"That was incredible," he whispered, kissing the top of her head.

"Yeah, it was." She tried not to think, tried to force the momentary peace she had felt, that post-sex euphoria that had filled her with a brief glow, to return; tried to hold on to the pleasure of his skin against hers. Tried to block out the steadily loudening voices of uncertainty and disquiet that had been rising in the eight days since their reunion.

Already she could feel his breathing slowing as sleep began to steal him away, and when he spoke again it was with the tone of one whose drowsiness would soon win over. "Happy New Year, Melissa."

"Happy New Year, Michael."

His gentle snores came soon after, his whole body relaxed yet still holding her. Melissa's peace was gone, though. She lay in the dark, staring at the stars through the windows that hadn't been concealed by the curtains, and listening to him as he slept. She lay there for hours, feeling empty, hollow. Feeling lost again. She waited for sleep to claim her as it had claimed the man who shared her bed. She was forced to wait a long time.

The dream of drowning in thick, syrupy dark water didn't evaporate as she opened her eyes, the sensation of not being able to breathe causing her to bolt up in her bed, hands going to her throat. She has kicked the bed covers off sometime during the night and she should have felt even a little cold. But her naked body had no goose bumps over its surface; had no reason to – it was stiflingly warm.

Retrieving her dressing gown from where she had draped it over the chair in front of her vanity table, she wrapped it around herself as she walked to the radiator. She wasn't cold; she just wanted to cover up. She didn't have to touch the metal surface; even with her fingers an inch away she could feel the heat that encompassed it.

After visiting the bathroom, she went downstairs and stood in front of the thermostat in the hallway. It had been raised, set to twenty degrees. More than a little pissed off at the increase, Melissa turned it back to the fourteen she always had it set to.

"Michael?"

She walked into the empty living room, started to cross the floor to head to the kitchen where she could hear movement, and stopped dead. Anger growing, she turned to her right, looking straight at the wall behind her sofa; a wall that had, when she and Michael had gone to bed last night, been bare.

"It looks good, don't you think?"

As he spoke from the doorway behind her, Melissa continued to look at where her Salvador Dali painting now hung. "What the hell is this, Michael?"

"You said that's where you were going to hang it, so I figured I'd save you a job."

The amused tones in his voice only increased how angry she felt, and she vied to keep hold of her temper. "I said I *thought* that that was where I was going to hang it. I hadn't decided properly. And I also said that *I* was going to hang it, when I eventually *did* decide."

"Well, I woke up earlier and couldn't get back to sleep." It seemed that he had noticed her displeasure and the amusement had left his voice, replaced with sulkiness. "I don't see what the big deal is."

"No, you wouldn't," Melissa muttered quietly under her breath before turning to him, clenched fists hidden in the pockets of her dressing gown. "The big deal, Michael, is that it's my home. You shouldn't have done that without asking me first." He started to speak, but Melissa continued before he could. "Like the way you should have asked me before turning the heating up. You know that I can't stand it being too warm, which is why it's set to the temperature it is."

"I was cold." The grousing was clearer in his voice, along with a glint of hostility.

That glint chased her own anger away; it worried her in a way that was very close to actual fear. She didn't want this to end up in a confrontation. "Michael," she said, her voice quieter. "You just need to ask before you do stuff like this, okay?"

He nodded and slouched back into the kitchen, that sliver of stone still clear in his dark blue eyes. He called out to her as he continued to make breakfast for himself. "What did you want to do today?"

"Well, I need to visit my mother later this morning, so…"

There was a heavy pause, Melissa could almost feel the weight of it. "Okay. We can have breakfast, then I'll get out of your way."

Despite the sullenness of his barbed reply, Melissa sighed

silently. The lie had come out without any planning, and she was glad that he had accepted it without question. She had no intention of going to her mother's flat – she just wanted some space, some time alone, without Michael being around.

* * *

The almost solid fog rendered her keen and piercing eyes worthless. The tall trees that she knew were all around her were only vague shapes that occasionally loomed up before her. But it didn't stop her padded paws from pushing her onwards, racing her through the forest.

A simple strain of confusion filled her animalistic mind. She had run from this place, run from the storm that had filled the wood with its threatening air. Had found a new path and had journeyed down it with prevailing freedom. But, somehow, she had wound up back in the wood that she had known for so long.

Her eyes revealed nothing but shadows and she had to rely on her nose to lead her through the maze of trees. But the fog seemed to be distorting the scents, watering them down; she recognised the trail of the area, the familiar aromas – even traces of her own scent on the ground. But the thick moisture-locked mist confused it all. Several times she had to change course in an instant, barely in time to stop herself from colliding into a tree or catapulting herself over a fallen log. Yet still she ran at her fast rate, refusing to slow.

The night outside the fog darkened as the hours passed onwards, the wolf still running through the night. Her thundering paw-steps began to decelerate, and panic gnawed through her. Her strong and muscled legs began to feel weak and atrophied, the power that she had always had in her limbs fading. It wasn't long before she was forced to stop completely, her body trembling with exhaustion.

She whirled around in circles, trying to peer everywhere. Her eyes had lost their sharpness just as her body had lost its strength. The mist-muted smells were now imperceptible; she couldn't pick up the slightest trace. Panic was moving through her as she lost all sense of her lupine nature, twirling in ever more chaotic circles. Without warning, she was falling, her paws scrambling at the embankment for some purchase.

Yelping as she hit the water, the fog not touching the surface of the red waters she now struggled in, pain sank into her. Fighting against the slow water movements she at last managed to get herself the right way up. As she caught sight of her dim reflection in the dark water, she felt the world disappearing into confusion, even the pain from the water she stood in was fading. She howled to the night, a sound that was a strange fusion of animal and human.

She looked like a monster. Stretching out from her furred neck, the lupine head changed before the ears. Where a wolf's face should have been, complete with a snout and a strong muzzle, there was now a human face. Melissa's green eyes stared out from those hairless features, eyes wide and terrified. As her mouth opened again to emit that combined howl-scream, wolf's teeth decorated her human gums.

She woke up sobbing, the pillow beneath her wet from tears she'd cried during her troubled dream. In the dark, she held her right hand close to her face, expecting to see a paw blanketed in grey and brown fur instead of her own smooth light skin-covered hand.

The part of the bed beside her was empty. She had slept alone for the first time in seventeen days. Michael had been a constant guest every night since they had got back together, leaving only to go to work and then returning each evening. Yesterday, Melissa had asked him to stay at his place, reasoning that with her appointment with Andrew being so early in the morning it just made more sense. He had accepted it, though his manner had cooled considerably towards her afterwards. What he didn't know, and what she had no intention of ever telling him, was that she had cancelled the appointment while he was at work the day before.

She ignored the clock. There was no reason for her to look at it. Her own body told her that she hadn't had even close to enough sleep, yet she also knew that her mind would not allow her to go back to sleep. Flashes of her dream played out as she grabbed her quilt and walked down the stairs with it. The light chased away the darkness from the living room when she flicked the switch, and she dumped the cover on to the sofa. Having chosen a DVD of a fantasy film, she settled underneath the cover with a drink in hand. Melissa watched the film without watching it, hearing it without taking in a single word, and just started to wait the hours out.

The DVD had returned to the menu screen, the drink she still held was stone cold, and harsh daylight filtered in through the curtains when Melissa opened her eyes. She had no memory of falling asleep, had no memory of even feeling tired, or of her eyes closing. Her head ached, her neck stiff from the way her head had fallen against the back of the sofa.

The light hurt her eyes and as she walked to the kitchen she turned it off, wincing at the sound of the switch being flicked. Even emptying her cup into the sink caused the pain in her head to flare up, her stomach rolling. The cup slipped from her hand, jagged red lightning striking her brain as it clattered in the metal basin, and she leant over it. Her hands automatically caught her hair, pulling it back in case she did need to vomit. The queasiness she felt quietened when she stopped moving, when the change in stature ceased to send a pounding pressure crashing through her head.

When she was completely sure that the danger had passed, she stood back up straight, moving slowly to ensure that the pain wouldn't return. Still moving carefully, she took out a pack of ibuprofen caplets from one of the drawers and popped two out of the blister pack. She started to put them away, then paused. Past experience told her that there was no way that the two tablets that sat in the palm of her left hand were going to even touch the blinding migraine. It was incredibly stupid, and she knew that it was, but also knowing that she couldn't cope with the pain of it any longer, she pushed another two out to join the others.

Tipping her head up to take the tablets made her feel close to passing out, yet the water that washed them down was so cool on her throat, trickling down to her stomach, that it did make her feel a little better.

Carrying the quilt up the stairs, holding one edge and dragging it up the steps behind her, used up the little energy she had. For an instant, she was flung back into her dream, back to that moment when her strong wolf body started to lose its potency. Her body tried to force that same panic she had felt back in on her, but the one positive thing about her migraine was that it protected her from everything else, not allowing anything but the pain in.

Lying on the bed, pulling the cover over herself and waiting for the motion sickness she felt from becoming horizontal to pass, Melissa closed her eyes, praying that when she opened them again both the pain and the nausea would be gone.

* * *

Melissa tore the envelope open, expecting the worst but hoping for the best. Her address was written in her own handwriting and the A4 envelope was too heavy not to contain the material she had submitted, but still there was that hope.

Her hands were trembling slightly as she removed all of the contents but she didn't glance at any of the covering letter until she had put her returned poems onto the sofa beside her. Then, after a deep breath, she looked at the letter.

It was a standard typed rejection letter, her name having been written in by hand after the black typed 'Dear'. It was the same as the ones that she had received when she was younger, just worded differently: 'I read your poems with interest' and 'unfortunately, I do not believe them to be right for our publication', and not forgetting the ever present 'I hope you are able to find a suitable publication'.

The message that had been scrawled at the bottom of the letter, in the same blue writing that her name had been written in, eased the disappointment that settled in her stomach. *I'm sorry that I am unable to accept your poems for publication in our magazine – they're simply not the right subject matter. But I wanted to add that I found them wholly enjoyable to read, brilliantly structured, passionate, and beautifully honest. I truly hope you find somewhere suitable for your talent to be seen.*

She read it a couple of times and each time she did the initial disappointment lifted a little bit more. She'd had a number of rejection letters when she used to submit her poetry when she was younger, but this one was, by far, the best! Although she wished that it said 'we'd love to publish your poems and we will pay you hundreds of pounds', it was still so much better than a 'thanks, but no thanks'.

Melissa settled back to finish drinking her coffee, ignoring the other two letters she'd received. The first one was just a bank statement and she was fairly sure that the other was a bill – and they could both wait a couple of hours to be opened.

After her lunch, as she sat with a pad of paper on her lap and jotted down a couple of ideas for a new poem, her phone rang. She looked at the display to see Michael's number flashing out. She paid no attention to it, resolutely staring at the paper, knowing that her mobile would soon emit its song. When it did, she simply closed her eyes and waited for it to stop.

What he'd said the other day still irritated her, still hurt her, and she was in no mood to either get into another argument or pretend that everything was okay.

The Friday after her unattended appointment with Andrew he had, once again, been at her house. The Wednesday night that she had spent by herself, in her nightmarish dream-state and then encased in her nightmarish pain, had been the only night that she had been alone.

Michael had been reading the sports pages of the local newspaper and Melissa sat beside him, scanning through the three pages of jobs. There were a few vacancies that had grabbed her attention and she'd circled them with a red pen. Most were simple secretarial work, one just a typist/filing job. They were duties that she had done before while working as a personal assistant, but none that would put her under too much strain – in other words, just what she needed.

Without looking up, Michael spoke, almost distractedly. "I don't know why you're bothering."

She looked at him. "What do you mean?"

He smiled, the meanness in it, Melissa realised, she was very used to seeing. Yet he still didn't look up from the pages he was reading. "Well, no one's going to hire you, are they?" He laughed cruelly. "Come on, Melissa! Be realistic for once! Who the hell's going to hire someone who is under psychiatric care for trying to kill herself?!"

He hadn't even looked up when she'd walked out of the living room with tears prickling her eyes.

Sighing, she picked up her mobile when it beeped to tell her that she had a new text message. She slid her phone closed after deleting his inquiry as to her whereabouts without replying. She'd talk to him later.

Trying to write after that was pointless; she couldn't concentrate and her good feelings faded. Resignedly, she put her writing things away and started to make herself another drink. She stared out of the kitchen widow, looking as the rain obscured everything as it fell heavily and quickly. The weather had turned the world dark, but this actually picked up Melissa's spirits; she'd always preferred the rain to sunlight.

Smiling, she switched off the kettle before it could boil completely and rinsed the coffee grounds from her cup. She put a towel in the hallway next to the front door, threw on her trainers and thin waterproof coat and left the house.

She walked the two minutes before her private road met the main road, moving onto the pavement. Although there was a hood on her jacket, she hardly ever used it; the feeling of the water cascading over her was too refreshing to be denied, like being reborn. It had been one of the few pleasures she'd had as a child, and one of the few things that had never changed or had lost any of its magic.

Walking along the path towards the centre of the village, looking at the houses she passed, set so far back from where she was, their gardens huge and almost perfectly maintained, she revelled in the stillness around her. She'd always felt that she must be the only person to love walking in the rain. Certainly, whenever she had listened to people complaining about the British weather and added that she preferred it raining, there had, so far at least, never been anyone who had agreed with her. Instead, they'd always looked at her in good humour but also in a way that suggested that she must be ever so slightly mad! And, given how invigorating she found it to be, Melissa was actually inclined to agree!

It washed away all of her thoughts of problems and confusion, it cleared her mind of all troubles. Plus the emptiness of the world helped – she'd always felt better with fewer people around her, more comfortable with her own company than with other people's.

Melissa returned home over an hour later, her hair drenched, her trainers and socks and feet wet from the mass of water that had soaked through, her jeans water-logged and twice as heavy as they had been when she had set out. In the hallway, with the door securely locked, she stripped off completely, letting her sodden clothes fall into a heap. She wrapped the towel around her, but not before a chill hit her.

As she ascended the stairs, she towelled herself dry. Once in her bedroom, she exchanged the towel for her dressing gown. After drying her hair and dumping her towel and her soaked clothes into the washing machine, she made herself a hot chocolate – treating herself to a couple of marshmallows which she added to the dark drink – before settling on the sofa, lounging on it with her legs tucked up beside her. Looking at the letter she had gotten, a shot of happiness flitted through her.

There was another message from Michael on her mobile phone. Sighing, she picked up the letter that had made her feel so happy despite it being a rejection, and took it up to her room. A pang of sadness struck her heart as she hid it, folded up, in the back of the book of her own poetry, and hid them both away in her wardrobe.

"What the fuck do you mean, I should have asked you?!" Her face was red, adrenalin was streaming through her and she was trembling from the effort of trying to control herself. On the dining room table her poetry book had been thrown into its centre, sending some of the loose leaves skidding across its surface and cascading others to the floor. The letter that had started the argument was folded again and held securely in Melissa's tight grasp, the creases that worked over it were clear; creases that had been formed when Michael had screwed it up and thrown it at her after he had discovered while looking, without her permission, through her things.

"You should have asked me if it was okay to send them off, to let somebody else read them!" He stood with his arms crossed across his chest, the muscles taunt.

Melissa looked at him, her mouth opened slightly, her total disbelief at what he was saying defusing her anger – but only for a moment. Just the feel of the paper in her hand, the fingers touching over the creases that he had put there, was enough to keep her vexation close to boiling point.

"I'm supposed to ask you?" She was aware of the power escaping her eyes, could feel them blazing as the thin string of her temper began to fray. "You actually think I need to ask you for *permission* to send my own poems off for publication?"

He just looked stubbornly back at her, arms still folded, not answering.

"You actually think," she continued, stepping slowly forwards, "that I have to ask you for permission to do *anything*?! It has got NOTHING to do with you what *I choose to do*! If I want to send my poems off, I can do that! If I want to spend time alone, I can do that! And if I want to walk through the fucking streets naked, I can do that too, without FUCKING HAVING TO ASK FOR YOUR FUCKING PERMISSION!"

The last word was barely spoken, the final syllable barely sounded, before she hit the ground on her hands and knees. Tears had filled her eyes the instant that his hand had collided with the side of her face as he backhanded her, sending a cold numbness from just underneath her eye socket to the bottom of her jaw. A second later, the numbness vaporised into white pain, her vision obscured by the spiralling white lights that now seemed to fill the room. Nausea grabbed her as she was roughly brought back to her feet, his fingers digging into the flesh and deep into the muscle of her upper arms as he lifted her up off the floor.

His tone was flat and calm as he pulled her close to his face. "From now on, you ask me before you do anything."

His eyes were just as emotionless as his voice, completely devoid of any semblance of emotion, not even the anger that he had shown when he had walked in and slammed the small black book onto the table. But although his eyes were empty of emotion, they were far from empty. There was a calculation in his eyes, a personal deceit. It was the look that her father had always had in his eyes, each time; it was the look of someone who was trying to justify to himself that he was doing nothing wrong.

And she had had enough! Each atom of anger that she had bitten back over the years, each little bramble of self-hatred for what she had allowed others to do to her, the humiliation that she had taken sole responsibility for, now found an outlet. The accumulation of every negative impulse that she had denied herself swelled to fill her. With the print of the back of his hand still blooming across her cheek, with his hands still pressing on her arm and his fingertips still bruising the skin, she focussed that potent ire into one movement.

She expelled fifteen years of pent up fury as she swiftly brought her knee forcefully into his groin.

He hit the floor in an instant, Melissa only just managing to shake his grasp off before he was able to pull her to the floor as well. An inkling of guilt tickled through her as she looked at the sudden change of the colour of his skin, the grey flesh speckled with beads of sweat. He leant over his legs, his forehead almost touching the carpet, with his hands now clasped around the hot ball of pain where she had contacted.

But she could still feel the ache in her face, and the paper she still held had crumpled again, her hands automatically having clenched when he had struck her. Warily, she moved a little closer to him, moving close enough to feel the heat that now rose from him like a fever. She spoke strongly, her voice filled with confidence and loud enough so that he would be able to hear over his agonised groans.

"You are never going to hit me again, Michael. You are never going to *touch* me again. I don't want to hear from you, I don't want to see you. You are going to scramble to your feet, or crawl if you have to – I really don't care which – and you are going to get *out of my house, and out of my life*!"

He made no response but he managed somehow to get to his feet. He stood for a moment, swaying drunkenly on the spot and his head hanging almost to his chest. His nose was running and he raised one hand to wipe underneath it, replacing his hand protectively over his crotch. He said nothing, just hobbled around Melissa and walked from her sight.

As she heard his car revving loudly before wheel-spinning as he accelerated away, she lifted her hand and held it to the burning area on her cheek and jaw. She slowly sank to the floor and just stared at the carpet, seeing the individual fibres that made up the whole. When she started to cry, she wasn't sure if the sounds that accompanied the tears were sobs or hysterical laughter.

Melissa sat on the step outside the back door, a large glass of vodka and coke in her hand. It was cold, but not bitterly so, the clouds shading the stars and keeping the temperature above freezing. The huge measures of alcohol she'd had helped to keep the cold at bay.

It had been dark when she had returned home from the police station, after nervously going in and speaking to the desk sergeant. In a little side room she'd given a statement, going into as much detail about her history with Michael as she could and recounting everything that had happened that night. It was witnessed by an officer who had asked her whether she wanted to press charges. She had given it serious thought for, what seemed to her at least, a long time, while the officer sat and looked at her. He had nodded, disappointedly but expectantly, when she said no, that she just wanted the situation on record. She began to explain that she hoped that he would now leave her alone, but he had accepted her answer straight away; it was a scenario that he had sat through many times before.

She had sat on the step as soon as she'd arrived home, alternating between a glass of vodka and coke, and two glasses of water. The side of her face, now a rainbow of dark bruises, ached badly and she wanted to take some painkillers to ease it to a comfortable level. But the alcohol was doing more that just keeping away the cold; it was doing a great job of easing her pain, too, and it was a hell of a lot more enjoyable to take than tablets!

Her head was swimming dizzily as she looked at the dark garden before her, listening to the quiet, the blessed solitude that once again filled her world. She knew that it had been stupid, allowing Michael back into her life in the first place, a mistake to ignore the doubt that had plagued her so many times, but now she could enjoy the peace that came from being alone. And the bruises on her face and arms would serve her as a temporary reminder; and the memory of the bruises would serve much longer.

Her balance was a little wavery as she eventually locked the back door and, holding onto the rail for support, made her way upstairs.

Half-heartedly, she brushed her teeth and, heeding the slight grumblings of her stomach, put her hair up into a ponytail; she knew that with the amount of drink she had had, she would be very lucky to get away without being sick.

She felt like she was being ripped apart inside. Tears ran down her face as she retched, the stench of bile battling for supremacy against the underlying stink of the alcohol as it forced its way out of Melissa's system.

Even with her eyes open she could see the images from the dream that had woken her. She and Michael had been having sex, moving as they had done so many times before in the waking world. She could feel him above her, hearing his laboured breath. Then it wasn't Michael pinning her arms to the bed beneath them, wasn't Michael breathing in her ear. It was her father.

She had opened her eyes, sobbing loudly, and ran to the bathroom with her hands clamped to her mouth. She managed to get there, managed to lift the toilet seat and position herself before it just in time.

There was nothing left, though now. She knelt before the toilet, heaving, her skin dripping with perspiration and tears. As feverish as her skin felt, she still shivered with cold. She reached out and pulled the handle down, flushing away everything she had brought up, and slumped against the wall near the radiator, trying to sit in any way that would lift the pain in her stomach.

Minutes passed while Melissa tried to slow her breathing down, trying to control the stitches that had taken hold of her strained sides. On trembling legs she moved to the sink and brushed her teeth almost violently, using the brush on the surface of her tongue as she hoped to get rid of the taste that was in her mouth and throat.

She sipped a little bit of water, just a little, and tried to fight it. But it was just too much. Hastily, she flung open the medicine cabinet, knocking things around on the shelves. She couldn't see them! Furiously, she hit things out of her way, the small room filled with the sound of things crashing into the sink and bouncing into the bath; her tweezers, her body sprays, all being pushed every way in her search for her scissors, but she couldn't see them! Sobbing in desperation, Melissa scanned the empty shelves then looked down at the scattered debris. In the midst of boxes of plasters and beauty products, she spied them and picked them up, almost impaling her hand on one of the blades.

She didn't hold back, *couldn't* hold back. The cuts weren't especially deep but they were long and many in number. Bleeding from both of her exposed arms wasn't enough and she put her scissors down long enough to slip out of her jeans before continuing her self-mutilation on the fresh skin.

Her head seemed to float off into the air high above her, and she had just enough time to drop the scissors back into the sink before it took her over. Luckily missing both the toilet bowl and the bathtub, Melissa collapsed into a heap on the carpeted floor.

Chapter Twelve

The coffee tasted foul and she put it down onto the table, grimacing at the persistent taste. She'd taken some tablets but the pain in her head was still lingering within reach and her throat felt shredded. The swelling on the right side of her face where Michael had struck her had gone down but a new, smaller bump had appeared on the left temple. Melissa guessed that it had happened when she had collapsed, and she praised her luck that she had hit nothing more than the soft floor. She speculated about the chance of concussion, but as she was able to focus easily and consistently, she was willing to take the chance that it wasn't one of the problems she had.

Before putting her dressing gown on Melissa, had cleaned her cuts up and used her antiseptic cream but hadn't covered them; there was something that she needed to do before she concealed them, if, that was, she had enough plasters to even do that. With the acknowledgement that the coffee would not improve in taste, she left it and walked to the bedroom.

She opened her curtains and took a moment to look at the dark clouds that littered the sky, the strong winds pushing them along. Sighing, she walked to her vanity table, stepping back enough so that she could see from the top of her head down to just below her kneecaps. Eyes closed, she slipped her dressing gown from her soft shoulders and let it pool around her feet. Then she raised her eyes and looked at her reflection.

How was it possible for the damaged girl looking back at her to actually *be* her? Bruises radiated out over her face, one half of her lip slightly swollen, the eye blackened, and the bump on her temple had darkened the area of the skin directly around it. She lowered her eyes and took in the identical five-dot patterns on the top of her arms. On her lower arms she saw the five-month-old scars, and on the other side her arms screamed out with the mesh of red lines that she had inflicted upon herself last night. Her stomach rolled painfully, emptily. Her pale stomach was clear of marks, clear of scars, as was her chest and breasts. But below the small nest of her pubic hair, only centimetres from her bikini line, the cuts continued like bleeding cracks over porcelain.

She looked for a long time. Each time she found herself turning away she forced herself to keep looking at those cuts. She saw the deep sadness in her eyes, the hollowness that she had seen not long before she had decided to end her life. In comparison to the fresh cuts, the scars along her wrists were dull but she could still see them clearly. If she continued down the old familiar route, then how long would it take until she tried to reopen those old wounds?

The wind blew her hair backwards and tried to gain purchase on her dressing gown as she stepped outside, but she was quick enough to catch a hold of it before she flashed her otherwise naked body to the dark morning world. She nearly dropped her small notebook and pen in her haste to stop exposing herself to the garden, but she was able to rearrange her hands so that she could both hold the book and keep her dressing gown closed.

She bathed herself in the sensation of the wind hitting her while she sat in her usual spot. The paving made her feet cold but she rested them on the ground anyway. Even though she still held the two objects in her hands, she felt them no more than she felt the cold ground on her soles. All she felt was the chilled winds against her face, billowing her hair towards the house.

She absorbed the breeze, took the raw freshness of it into herself and could feel it building up into something powerfully intense. She recognised the almost mystical sense in her body, moving along and burning through her veins, that impending surge of inspiration. Much like the build-up of her desire to cut, she felt the itch to pick up her pen grow stronger; but like the desire to cut, she refused to give in for a moment. With her eyes closed, she dwelled in a dark world where the rush of the wind matched the rush of creativity – that call for her to give in.

When she clicked her ballpoint pen and opened the notebook the scratchings she made with her red pen were little more than scrawls, but she couldn't move slowly. The dam of her inspiration had broken and she couldn't slow the flood. There were no hesitations in her writings, the flawlessly right words presenting themselves automatically, her heart singing out in silent speech everything that ached within. As she filled pages with her almost illegible markings, she only crossed out one line of words, replacing it underneath with the 'correct' ones, and two other similarly imperfect additions.

Tears had started to fall from her eyes, but as she clicked the pen to retract the nib she couldn't decide if she was sad, happy, or empowered. Now that the fever of her creativity had passed, leaving her feeling a little empty, she was able to write slower and more controlled, the writing a lot neater as she copied her newest poem out again in her notebook, mainly to make it easier for her to read. While she did, she smiled, feeling the words taking her over.

The Choice
A whispered sigh,
A shifting breeze.
Sweeping through my soul and heart.
A cooling breath
Upon warm skin
Takes me backwards to the start:
Before the sting,
Before the grief,
Before the pain engulfed the dream;
When life to live,
All hopes attained,
Was just as simple as it seemed.
Choices easy,

Games well played,
The future would sort itself.
Dreams of fortune,
Of love and joy
Guaranteed, success and wealth.
But life of pain,
Of trust betrayed,
Smashed those dreams to foolish dust,
Childish pretence,
Inane charade,
Ruined, corroded through to rust.
Too long I lay
In surrender,
Destroyed by those from the past;
Permit their deeds
To hold me there,
Chase all those hopes to the last.
But as I stand
Before that breeze,
Cooling in the autumn heat,
Sun descending
Far in the west,
My heart sounds out a stirring beat.
That silent cry,
The voice within,
Begins to rise to a shout.
Its silent words
Unheard till now,
Once trapped behind fear and doubt,
Scream upwards to
The red-stained sky,
As the winds begin to blow:
The breeze transformed
Into a gale,

Lifts me where pain cannot go.
The stormy winds
'Waken once more
Strength to be, to stand, to fight,
To push aside
All that has been
And banish it out of sight.
The wind within,
The wind without
Are one and the very same
And neither one
Of the wild storms
Can ever again be tamed.
For my soul
And grieving heart
Hear the words sung in the storm:
"Learn from the past,
Wield lessons well
In sight of the future dawn.
Bear arms of strength
Of steadfast drive
To become all you can be;
To move from pain,
From strife and grief,
To greet your life, whole and free.
Do not give in,
Don't wait and dream,
Don't sit and bewail your fate;
Begin to fight
Or learn to fail:
The choice is yours to make!"

* * *

It had been their first session since before Yule and Melissa had only just managed to fill Andrew in on everything that had happened in the short hour of their meeting. She had talked about the time spent with her mother, about the confusion due to her obvious attempts in improvement; of getting back together with Michael; going to her sister's graveside; and she explained exactly why she had cancelled the last appointment with him. She went into the details of the fight with Michael and, shame-faced, her reaction to the dream she had had.

He had looked at the six-day old bruises on her face that had turned from red and purple to green and yellow. He had looked at the five-day old gashes on her arms with the same expression. He had studied each long and short red line, those that crossed each other and those that were apart from the rest, and had listened as she explained that her legs were in a similar state.

Melissa had seen the disappointment in his eyes, which had reshaped to cautious optimism as she talked. Although doubt had still been there, Andrew had been pleased by her poem, and even more pleased when she told him that a copy of it was taped to the cupboard above her kettle so that she would see it every day. She had reassured him that she was okay with the appointments staying fortnightly and not reverting to weekly as they had been in September. He hadn't been overly convinced, but had at least accepted that she wasn't going to be swayed – especially after promising that she wouldn't skip another appointment.

Driving home it had become clear to her just how much she still needed a psychiatrist to talk to. Being able to offload all of the events, all of her feelings and thoughts, without worrying about upsetting him or fearing about his reactions.

Melissa was lost in her own little world as she parked the car in front of the house, the mass of thoughts that still conflicted in her mind as she speculated over exactly *how* she was going to start building – *re*building – her life. Her thoughts of possible futures stopped when she walked through the front door. She only closed it in an automatic reaction; her attention was fixed on the single red rose that lay on the bottom step of the flight of stairs.

She realised that the overwhelming scent of roses that she'd detected as soon as she'd stepped in couldn't have come from that single one flower, and she followed the aroma to the living room.

Roses covered the mantelpiece, lying along it in large bunches. They covered the dining table and rested against the legs of the chairs. Long stemmed flowers rested against the TV and on top of it, and hundreds of loose petals were strewn upon the floor.

Things started to click into place as she picked up her phone. After consulting her address book, she dialled the number for her local police station.

"You didn't give him a key?"

Melissa shook her head. "No. But I think I've figured out how he got in."

The middle-aged officer sat with his notepad out, jotting down the information she gave him. He raised his eyebrows, indicating for her to continue.

"I think he stole my spare keys when we broke up in November. After I told him it was over he smashed a cup against the wall, and when he went into the kitchen to look for something to clean it up with I heard my keys being moved. I think that night was the last time I saw them until the night we got back together. When he found them. Under the fridge, he said. I thought it then, but now I'm nearly sure: I looked under the fridge when I noticed they were missing."

The officer finished jotting it all down. "So you think he took your keys and made a copy?"

"Yes."

"Phil?"

Both Melissa and the police officer, whose first name was Philip, turned to the doorway. The plain-clothed officer who stood there held another single long stemmed rose and a small rectangle white card in his gloved hand.

"These were on her bed." He met them halfway, in the middle of the living room floor and turned the card around for them both to see.

Melissa read it aloud. "'Take me back.'"

"Melissa, you said that you'd phoned the locksmith. Sorted to get your locks changed?"

She nodded, still looking at the card and flower that Michael had put on the place where she slept. "Yeah. Both my front and back doors. They said someone would be here soon."

The officers exchanged a look that Melissa didn't see, and the uniformed officer sighed. "Well, we'll be leaving someone here until then."

Melissa nodded again. She was so glad that he had said that.

* * *

They'd managed to track him down at work the day after he'd been at Melissa's house, leaving her his little tokens; and they hadn't been cheap, either! They'd taken him to the station and questioned him. He'd been allowed to leave after receiving an official caution, and with the strong advice not to contact or visit 'Miss Adams' again. They'd also pinched the key to her house as evidence. He had thought he had been clever, making two copies of the key; but when he had tried the other copy when Melissa had briefly gone out this morning, it didn't work. She'd changed the locks on him!

Twenty-eight hours after being ordered to stay away, Michael sat outside Melissa's house, concealed behind a small bush, drinking can after can of lager and watching the windows. He watched as the lights were switched on when the darkness fell completely, and watched as the lights were switched off when Melissa went to bed.

Chapter Thirteen

Melissa sat there, feeling the treacherously loud booming of her heart beneath her smart, black blouse, the chair she sat in so alike the ones in the waiting room at the mental health clinic. She couldn't remember the last time she had felt so terrified! On the row of seats around her, lined up against the wall were six other women, all dressed as smartly as she was, all clasping folders of varying colours and sizes, as she was. There was one crucial difference, as far as Melissa could tell. Each one of them looked calm and collected; every one of them looked confident and stress free, and as if they belonged there.

The job had seemed so perfect to her on paper. The advert had listed the details for the typist position, with any candidates required to have a typing speed of at least sixty words per minute and preferable experience with the specified software. The software mentioned Melissa had had plenty of experience with when she worked as a PA, albeit an older version. Her typing speed had never dropped below eighty-five while she was working and she had been delighted to find out when she did an online typing test that she could still punch out seventy-three words per minute. Plus, the job hours seemed good as well; fifteen hours a week to be split over three days. The pay was a lot lower than she had been on at her previous job, but it was more than enough for her to live comfortably on; it wasn't as it she had a mortgage to pay, thanks to her late grandfather's generosity.

Two days after dropping off the application, Melissa had gotten a call from the head of human resources inviting her to an interview. So here she sat, on the fourteenth of March, watching as the other candidates were called in. When only she and one other woman remained, Melissa heard her name called.

Nervously, she smiled at the man in the suit and stood. Walking on legs that felt as if they would melt from underneath her, she followed him into the room.

"Have a seat, Miss Adams." The gentleman in the navy suit sat behind a large, and slightly cluttered, desk. There was a chair either side of him, the one on his left occupied by a youngish brunette in a fairly conservative ensemble. The man who called her in took the remaining empty seat. Melissa sat on the chair that faced them, crossing her legs neatly and resting her folder on her lap. She tried to portray an aura of self-assuredness, but doubted that she was pulling it off; not with her heart beating loud enough for the room to hear!

"There's no need to be nervous, Melissa." The woman's voice was quite low, and seemed to fit her perfectly.

"It's been a while since I've been in this kind of situation," Melissa said, laughing a little. "I'd forgotten how scary it is."

As they all chuckled companionably she felt a little of her nerves disappear.

"Well," said the man in the centre. "We'll try to make in as painless as possible. I'm William Morgan. This is Vincent Walsh and Lisa Harvey."

Melissa smiled at each of them. William glanced down at the papers before him, which Melissa assumed were her application forms, and saw identical papers before the other two as well.

"Okay. Well, first of all, the typing test you took this morning when you arrived. The results show your typing speed to be seventy-two words per minute, which is just one under what you said on your application. Which is, as you know, much more than we required."

Melissa could feel herself beaming. "When I was working in my former job it was in the mid-eighties; I was a little surprised that it was still as high as it is."

"It's impressive," Lisa added. "I'm lucky if I can type thirty words per minute!"

Melissa could feel herself relaxing more as they laughed again. It was obviously a very laid-back place.

"And the systems we mentioned? You said that you're familiar with them?"

"Yes. They're the main systems that we used at C. Taylor & Co. Well, the previous versions. The word-processing system was the eight-mark-three, I think. I can't remember the data-entry systems details. I would have to familiarise myself with them again, especially as they're the upgraded versions, but I can still remember the basics of their layouts."

The younger of the two men made a note on his copy of her application. "We contacted your reference, your former employer at C. Taylor. She spoke very highly of you. Said that you were a very hard worker, dedicated to the tasks set for you to complete, and that you weren't afraid to work on your own initiative and take charge. She also said that you were a very highly valued member of the team, and she had been very sorry when you'd decided that you had to leave."

"She was a lovely person to work for. Very understanding."

The two men looked at Lisa, who spoke; they had discussed that it would be more appropriate for the female member of the panel to inquire into the next subject.

"On your application, Melissa, you say that you left your previous employment due to personal problems. I hope you don't mind me asking, but would you mind going into more details?"

That invisible spotlight had returned after months of being gone. This was it, the moment she had dreaded most, the moment that she had obsessed over ever since thinking about applying. She had gone over her possible responses so many times in her mind, trying to find the best way to go into the details without freaking anybody out. Now that the moment was finally here, she found that every practiced and polished speech had flown out her head.

They were sitting there, staring at her, waiting for her to answer. Without a warning, her nervousness at the prospect of telling them disappeared; she decided to just go for it, and damn the consequences.

"I've suffered with depression on and off since childhood. The job began to get very stressful and I reacted badly, but as a part of my personal depressive response I didn't see any possible benefit in asking for help. My depression got worse and I quit my job. I ended up hurting myself badly, and have been seeing a psychiatrist since."

The awkward silence only lasted a moment but seemed to stretch on for much longer before William spoke. "When you said you hurt yourself badly, you mean…?"

"I attempted to commit suicide." She knew, especially with the startled expressions in their eyes, that she could not leave it there. "I know how extreme it sounds, and I also know that it isn't a flying endorsement for hiring someone; that somebody with a history of severe depression isn't high on an employer's list of candidates, as standard.

"I see a psychiatrist once a fortnight and he does not deem it necessary for me to be on any anti-depressant medication. I am working through the underlying causes of my depression, and am learning better ways of dealing with stressful situations so that I don't become so overwhelmed again. I've made a lot of improvements in my life, and things are getting easier for me all the time."

While the woman in the conservative suit and the younger man still looked at her uncomfortably, the older man had sat back a little in his chair, his lips turned up slightly at the edges.

"As you've seen from my application form, I am more than qualified to go back to a position more like the job I had at C. Taylor's, but I don't want to work in such a high-stress vocation; I don't want to undo all of the progress that I've made. I *know* that I can do this job, and I know that I can do it as well as, if not better than, the rest of the candidates that you'll see. I don't need to work, I could sit back and stay on the small amount of Incapacity Benefits I receive. But I *want* to work, and I know that

I'm ready to."

Even his colleagues grinned, if slightly uneasily, but William Morgan smiled openly. "Very well answered, Melissa."

She sighed in pleasure as she took off her high-heeled shoes, dropping them next to the sofa before lying along the cushions with her tight-clad feet hanging over the arm. She looked up at the ceiling, her arms beneath her head, grinning like an idiot.

She was relieved it was over, but more than happy that she had done it. After her little speech about the reasons for her leaving her previous employment, they had talked for a little longer, going over the specifics that the job would entail. They had given her the very strong impression that she had a good chance. Although she did hope that she would get the job, it really didn't matter if she didn't; she had done something positive. For now, that seemed enough.

Proof of the other step she had taken was standing beside the dining table in the form of her large suitcase. There were three nights left for her to spend in her own bed before she went away, but her anticipation of getting away from the house to sunnier climes had made her pack well before she needed to. The little bag that she would carry that contained her passport and tickets, along with the Euros that she would need, was in place next to the suitcase. Despite her guarantee to him that she wouldn't miss another appointment, Andrew had agreed that a holiday would be a good thing, and had allowed her to break her promise without making her feel guilty.

The strenuous warnings that Michael had received from the police seemed to have worked; she hadn't heard anything from him. But as her birthday had grown closer she started to think about how they had reconciled before. She didn't want him to turn up in five days' time on her birthday thinking that a gift would change things, as they had before.

It almost felt like running away, but she was keen to avoid any more contact with him. She didn't want contact to evolve into a confrontation. There was no proof that he would even bother with her – she hoped that he had forgotten all about her – but there was a warning playing at the base of her spine, so she had figured better be safe than sorry.

There were still the marks. Her legs and arms were healed now and, luckily, none of them had scarred, but she could still see the faint white lines where the skin had not yet hardened. Melissa was quite sure that she deserved a holiday.

Part of her just wanted to continue to lie down and ride the wave of her emotionally exhausted happiness, but another part felt like turning on a CD as loud as she could stand it, and just dance energetically around the house! She felt like, finally, she was doing something constructive.

* * *

There was no answer when he knocked and she must have changed both her house phone number and her mobile number. He continued knocking, standing there for five minutes – which he timed with his watch – but there was still no answer. She *had* to be there! Her car was parked three feet from where he'd pulled up in his; she just *had to be there*!

A storm brewing on his face, he stomped back to his car and started going through the boot. At the bottom, he found the electrical tape he'd been looking for, and went back to the front door. Savagely, he used the tape to secure the red rose and birthday card to the wood. That way, whenever she got back from wherever she *was*, she'd see his gift before she got inside.

Moodily, he threw the remainder of the roll of tape onto the back seat, threw the gear-stick into reverse and backed out of the drive, leaving wheel ruts in his wake.

* * *

The ferry touched back on British soil in the late afternoon, and the coach started its arduous journey North. Melissa sat in her plush seat, wishing that she were back on the ferry again, mainly because she hated not being able to stretch her legs.

Compared to the South of France where she had spent most of the ten-day holiday, the temperature as they moved steadily up the country plummeted deeply, and she only had the softly tanned skin to remind her that she had been somewhere warmer as the cold started to creep in.

The journey to the bus depot where she would end the coach trip took over five hours with all the different stops and drop offs. Gradually the seats started to empty and when they pulled up inside the depot with the multi-story car park built above, the coach was only a quarter full.

As she pulled her wheeled-suitcase along behind her, she passed through the pedestrian section of the bus depot and into the adjoining pedestrian section of the train station. Once outside, with the bitterly cold air hitting her like a sledge-hammer, she walked to the front of the long bank of black taxis.

Now that she was so close to home, she felt drained of all but the basic energy and thoughts. When she gave the taxi driver her address, when he took hold of her case and helped her in the back with it, it was only in a half-conscious daze. The cabbie chatted away amiably, contented enough for the odd affirmation from his passenger while he righted the wrongs of the world as he spoke. And Melissa just sat, aware enough to respond when response was necessary, but just happy to watch the night pass them.

In no time they were driving along the extended driveway and pulled up alongside her little car.

"Here we are, then," the driver said, getting out and helping her with her suitcase again.

He grinned and thanked her, almost ecstatically, when she told him to keep the change. She smiled herself at the over-enthusiastic gratitude that came from her giving him a twenty-pound note on a seventeen-pound fare.

As the car turned around in the drive it cast light over the otherwise dark house, and for a second it looked to Melissa like the setting of a horror story. It looked old, abandoned, full of dark secrets better not known. She could almost see the archetypal rolling mist from a thousand black and white movies surrounding it. And for that second, it was the last place she wanted to go. Then a cold breeze touched her back, sending an icy finger along her spine. She shivered, then sent laughter spilling out into the night.

The eerie darkness that she had sensed was gone, and it was just her home again, just the house that her father's parents had owned and her grandfather had left to her when he had died when she had been nineteen. It was the place that she had, despite its isolation, always felt safe. So, grabbing her suitcase by its much-used handle, she walked to the front door of her sanctuary, not noticing anything amiss as she passed her car. Because of the darkness around her, she was close to the entrance before she realised that there was something on her door, a slightly darker patch on the dark wood. Another step triggered the security light above the door.

She looked briefly at the envelope that had been stuck slightly askew, but it wasn't that which held her attention. The rose was clearly very dead, its petals curled and brown. Her fingers brushed against one, the crackle seemed very loud in the quiet, and she watched as a light shower of dried flakes speckled the ground.

"Michael," she whispered, sighing.

She let herself into the house, closing the door as gently as she could so as not to make any more of the flower fall – she wanted the police to see it as she had. She should probably ring them straight away, but she was too tired. From the look of those items, they had been there for a while and they would last for one more night; tomorrow would be fine.

But as tired as she was, there was something she had to do before she let sleep take her. She moved through the house, checking the windows and doors, and scanning the rooms quickly just to make sure that there had been no visitors inside while she had been away.

It was gone ten when she woke the next morning to the brightening March sky. When she first opened her eyes she felt disorientated. She wasn't in the bed that she had been in over the eight nights of her stay in the hotel, and it took her a moment or two to remember that she was back home. It brought with it the memory of what she had found when she had returned.

Ten minutes later, protected by her dressing gown and the trainers that she had slipped on over her bare feet and armed with a cup of coffee, Melissa walked outside. Although the slight breeze brought with it a cold splinter of rain on its way, the sun was warm on her tanned skin and for a moment she just basked in it, her eyes closed with the heat on her face.

The rose and what she now saw was a card had survived the night as she knew they would, and she was very tempted to forget the police and remove them from the door. But she left them where they were, and stepped away from the house, looking out at the drive. For a reason that she couldn't fathom, her eyes repeatedly worked their way back to her car, roaming over the slightly-dirty red paintwork. She couldn't pinpoint what was wrong, why she continually looked at the car, but she felt something definitely wasn't right; if she could only—

"That son of a bitch!" she whispered, very angry when her eyes finally caught on to what was wrong.

Both of the front tyres were totally flat at the bottom and when Melissa looked around the sides, she saw that both back tyres were in identical states. Without even having to look too hard she was able to see the huge gaping holes in between the treads. There was no doubt in her mind who was responsible.

"Fucking brand-new tyres, Michael." They were just over a month old. She'd had the old ones replaced at its last MOT; and they had cost a lot!

All of the relaxation of her holiday had evaporated without trace as she trudged back inside and picked up the card that the police had left her. As she dialled the direct line she had been given, she rubbed at her temples, hoping to stave off the headache that was trying to be born.

* * *

"Have you thought about getting an injunction against him? A restraining order or something?"

Melissa smiled at Andrew, and nodded. "Yeah, I've thought about it. I just don't know if it would do any good."

"Well, it would mean that he could be facing criminal charges if he comes near you again."

"I know. But it takes time to set it all up; it's got to go through the courts, a judge has got to decide if it's necessary, and even if it is, if he breaks it I have to be able to prove it. Plus, it might just make things worse."

Andrew laughed. "So, you *have* thought about it, then!"

"Yeah. The officer I spoke to when they came to see the damage he'd done to my car mentioned it. Talked me through the basics of it."

"Have they charged him for damaging your tyres?"

She shrugged. "No proof that it was him. I was gone for ten days; theoretically, anyone could have driven up to the house and stabbed my wheels."

"So, what happens now?"

"It's all been filed. With the birthday card he left me, they at least have proof that he ignored their warning. He's been warned again. I guess we just wait and see what happens."

"Talking of waiting and seeing…" he said with a good-natured glint in his eyes. "What about this job? Heard anything yet?"

"No, not yet. But they did say that they wouldn't be contacting anyone until at least next week. So..."

He sat back and regarded her with interest. "What do you think they'll say?"

"Honestly? I've been trying not to think about it too much!" She laughed, almost nervously. "I don't want to start obsessing over what I said, or what I didn't say, or what I could have phrased better. It's out of my hands now. But I think they'll consider me, at least. I think they'll look at my suitability to the job, and not discount me because I'm so obviously insane."

"We're all insane in one respect or another, Melissa. Some people are more obvious about it, that's all."

"Mmm. And some people are better at hiding it for a little longer." It was Michael's face that came to mind when she said that.

Andrew leant forward again. "Melissa, can I just say how proud of you I am?"

Melissa looked at him with her eyebrows raised, not one hundred percent sure that she'd heard what she thought she'd heard.

"You've managed to come *so far* in such a short space of time! I see a lot of people for a lot of different reasons, and there are people that I have been meeting with for years that haven't made as much progress as you have in, what...?"

"A little over seven months," she finished for him.

"There are so many people that I see, that I try to help, that have just given up. They talk constantly about bettering their individual situations, bettering *themselves*, but all they ever do is talk. They have no real desire, no real *drive*, to make the necessary changes in themselves. Although they know that things won't change unless they make it happen, they don't seem to know it deep down inside – so they just don't bother. They keep hoping that someone will come along with a quick and easy solution that doesn't require them to actually *do* anything!

"But you! Things keep getting thrown at you and, despite a couple of backward steps, you're leaping ahead."

"Fight or fail," Melissa whispered wistfully, smiling.

"Exactly!" Andrew shouted, and laughed. "I know it probably sounds a little patronising, but I am *so* proud of you, Melissa."

Happy tears welled up in her eyes. "It doesn't sound patronising at all. It means a hell of a lot to me for you to have said that. And besides," she said, wiping away the tears before they could fall. "I'm bloody proud of myself!"

When Andrew burst into surprised gales of laughter, Melissa joined in.

A number of thin wispy clouds drifted across the star-strewn black sky, and she stared up at the full moon. She had had to wait up until three in the morning before the moon had arched its way high enough so that she could see it from her back garden. She had waited, thinking of all of the different aspects of her life for which she could ask assistance. And only one thing seemed important enough.

She looked into the glowing face of the moon, the wondrous face of the silver goddess, and spoke. "Let them give me a chance. Let me prove to them, to myself, that I can do this again. Give me the chance to prove it."

* * *

One week and one day after April began, Melissa was halfway through her shower when the phone began to ring. Although she could have let the answer-phone get it – and given where she was, it would have been the sensible thing to do – Melissa nevertheless hurried out of the shower. With a towel wrapped around her body, and shampoo still lathered up in her hair, she rushed out of the bathroom and down the stairs, leaving wet footprints on her way.

She wiped her wet hands on her towel and answered the phone. "Hello?"

"Hello? I'm calling for Melissa Adams."

"Yes, speaking." She thought that she should recognise the woman's voice, but couldn't quite get it.

"Melissa, hi, it's Lisa Harvey, from Addison's."

Melissa's already racing heart from her flight down the stairs sped up. "Lisa, hi! How are you?"

"I'm fine, Melissa. How are you?"

"Not too bad, thanks."

"Good. Well, I have a bit of news about the job."

"Okay."

"Unfortunately, we're not able to offer you the position, Melissa."

"Oh." Her stomach plummeted and her heart felt very heavy.

"There was someone else who had more recent experience with the systems we use."

"It's okay, Lisa. I do understand. I'm just glad that you considered me at all."

"Melissa, although we can't offer you that position, there is something that we would like you to consider."

"Oh?"

"We have another position coming up, starting on the twentieth of May. It's almost identical to the one you applied for. It's a permanent position, same sort of duties – typing, data entry. It's the same money an hour, as well. The only difference is the hours. It's only twelve hours over the three days, instead of the fifteen hours. And we'd like to offer you that job. What do you think?"

Melissa closed her mouth, which had dropped open of its own accord while Lisa had been speaking. Now she opened it again.

"I think that sounds brilliant!"

"You don't have to give an answer straight away. You can take your time and think about it. I know that less hours means less money coming in, and—"

"Honestly, Lisa, I really don't need to think about it. It sounds brilliant; in fact, it sounds perfect."

"Excellent!" Melissa could hear the smile in the woman's voice. "Well, I'll send you all of the information and the contracts, so you can check all of it, make sure that everything's okay."

"Thank you very much, Lisa."

"Thank you, as well. You've just saved us from having to endure another interview process!"

Melissa laughed along with the woman who was soon to be one of her employers.

"Okay. Well, as I said, I'll send everything out to you, and I'll speak to you again soon. Any questions or problems, just let us know."

"Will do. And thanks again."

"You're welcome. Goodbye."

"Bye."

Melissa hung up and laughed aloud. She ran her hand through her wet hair, bringing a handful of soapy bubbles with it. Remembering that she was still only half way through her shower, she twirled quickly on the spot, laughing again (and almost losing her towel!) before running back up to the bathroom, screaming 'yes' repeatedly as loud as she could on her way up.

Chapter Fourteen

Exactly four weeks after the fantastic job offer, came the day that Melissa dreaded more than any other. The April showers had continued through to May, turning the ground into muddy swamps almost every day, and when Melissa woke on the morning of the sixth she heard the customary sound of the rain attacking the windowpanes.

Ten years.

It was the first thing that she thought when she opened her eyes, the first thing that made itself known in her mind. When four forty-five pm rolled around, when the afternoon started edging towards evening, it would be exactly ten years since her sister's life had ended, give or take a few minutes. And about fifty years or so before it should have.

There were no new thoughts or revelations, no new feelings – after ten years how could there be? But the anger and grief of those ten years still remained. This day was no different to any other day, really; just another day where her sister was still dead, still buried alongside the man who had killed her. The man who had been driving with his daughter when the police had tried to stop him. Maybe he had seen something on the cop's faces, disgust, maybe, aimed in his direction. Maybe it had been some keen instinct or intuition. Or maybe he just panicked out of guilt. It didn't matter what had caused it – the end result was really all there was. He had refused to stop, ignoring the flashing lights and siren of the car behind him, ignoring the startled cries of his eight-year-old daughter beside him.

He had raced through the streets, overtaking the cars that threatened to slow him down, forcing his way through the start of the rush-hour traffic. A lot of the time he was forced to drive on the white line as he overtook the cars that headed in the same direction, and making the cars moving towards him swerve dangerously to avoid head-on collisions. With the police still in pursuit, now in three cars instead of just one, Patrick Adams managed to manoeuvre himself to the nearest motorway junction – by pure luck rather than planning. There was so much more space, a lot fewer cars, and the vehicles that were spread over three lanes moved a hell of a lot quicker than the ones on the single-track roads he'd left behind.

As he travelled in the outer lane, occasionally having to undertake the cars that weren't quick enough to get out of his way, he saw the oncoming blue flashing lights again. The scattered traffic was slowing him down and he made his way back across the lanes. Riding on the hard shoulder made it so much easier and, still ignoring the confused sobbing from the seat next to him, he put his foot down on the accelerator.

Even pushing his car at ninety-five miles an hour, the police cars were right behind him. His glances into the rear-view and side mirrors as he tracked how far behind they were distracted him form the view ahead. He watched as one of the panda cars broke from the line and headed into the third lane, its speed increasing. He had seen enough car chases on the television to know that they were trying to box him in, so that they could force him to drop his speed and, ultimately, stop. He couldn't let them get in front of him, or it was all over.

Still watching the car that was coming up parallel to him, only three lands over, he increased the force on his own car's accelerator. The speed started to swell and he watched the needle on the speedometer move. He smiled a little before beginning to turn to Lauren, meaning to tell her to shut up – she had started to scream now instead of sob, and it was getting distracting.

He didn't even have time to face her. He had seen why her cries had turned to screams; she had seen it long before he had. There was no time to swerve, no time to even think about stopping. There wasn't even a full second for Patrick Adams to stare, petrified, at the broken-down car that blocked the hard-shoulder before it was too late. The car containing the man and his terrified child hit the blockage at ninety-seven miles an hour.

Melissa had learnt the details of the car chase from the local and national papers that had covered it, her imagination having supplied the things they couldn't possibly guess at. Although there had been no need to, some of the papers had sensationalised the story a little, but Melissa had been able to separate the facts from the over-dramatized tales. She knew that the motorway had been closed until the following day, that the hulks of twisted metal had lain where they had landed after impact, the second of which had blessedly been empty at the moment they'd collided. Both Lauren and Patrick had been killed straight away. Melissa was told that her sister would probably had felt little pain, that it would have been over before she could have suffered, and Melissa had no choice but to believe that. All she knew for sure was that she had not been allowed to see her sister afterwards, and that the coffin had been closed at the funeral.

Melissa got up and stood at the window, looking at the heavy downpour and the thick grey clouds that stretched to the horizon. It didn't look as though she'd be able to make it to the graveyard today.

The box that she had taken from the wardrobe the night before stood on top of the table, and drew her gaze continuously as she sat and drank her coffee. On the wall above her television were the four pictures that she had framed and hung. One was the school picture of herself and Lauren in their uniforms, and the other three were of Lauren alone. In the small periods of time when her eyes weren't fixed to the box filled with her past, they were fixed on those photos.

The plan had been to spend the day working her way through all of the box, not letting a single item go without looking at it, immersing herself in the memories of her sister's and her own childhood. But she just didn't think that she could face up to it today. Yet, still, it drew her attention.

* * *

"Why didn't you open it?"

"I don't know. I *wanted* to. I mean, I *really* wanted to. I just couldn't bring myself to go through everything."

"Why is it so important, though, Melissa? Why do you want to look through it so badly? And why is it so difficult for you to?"

"In that box is all I have of Lauren. Everything of hers that still exists is in there."

"And that sounds fine, Melissa. But I don't quite believe it's the real reason. Or, at least, I don't believe it's the *only* real reason."

"I'm starting to think you know a little too much about me, Andrew." She waited until he had finished chuckling. "You're right, though. It's not just all that's left of Lauren in there; all that's left of me is in there, too."

"What do you mean?"

"Despite the strong flaws in my character, I'm happy with the person I've become. Although I feel weak a lot of the time, I'm still here and I'm still struggling through. I'm a lot stronger than even I realise most of the time. But there is something missing, something *of me* that I lost somewhere."

"And you think you'll find it in there?"

"I think that, in there, I'll find out *what it is*, because I don't even know what's missing, let alone how to reclaim it."

"I still don't think I completely understand."

"Neither do I!" Melissa laughed. "I used to feel so sure of who I was when I was younger. Even when my life was at its worst, I still felt that it was okay because I was sure of myself. Things were always clear, always black and white. I knew what I had to do, because I knew myself, which made the choices very simple."

"Melissa, you like fantasy books, yes?"

She nodded, wondering about the abrupt change of topics.

"*Lord of the Rings*, *The Dark Tower* series by Stephen King? That sort of thing?"

"Yes."

"Do you know why people like books like that? The old good-against-evil genre, whatever the details of the story? Do you know why people are so drawn to them?"

"No."

Andrew leant forwards, a confidant about to share a great and powerful secret. "Because they make things simple."

Melissa frowned. "I don't know what—"

"Okay. *Lord of the Rings*: they have one task, only one. They have to battle across the darkness and the fires to destroy an item that would mean the end of them. They have a very simple choice – they keep going or they give up. But why is it so simple? Because while on that task, when they only thing that matters is to find a way to banish the evil that spreads across the land, that *is* all that matters. They don't have to worry about the mundane everyday stress of life. They don't have to worry about housework, about paying rent or a mortgage, of working, or paying the bills. It's simple because *surviving* is all that they have to worry about. You see?"

She smiled. "So, I'd probably be more content if I were fighting for my life against unspeakable evil?"

"'Content' is probably the wrong word." He laughed along with her. "But it would take away all of the excess stresses that come with life. It takes you back to your childhood, when paying bills and having all of those 'grown-up' issues to deal with were just impossible to imagine; when living was all there was."

"So, what I'm looking for isn't exactly my inner child; it's more of my inner-Hobbit."

"I guess it is!"

It took a long time for Andrew and Melissa to stop laughing at that image, laughing fully in surprise, the way you can't prevent when something turns out to be a lot funnier than you'd planned it to be.

"Okay." Melissa wiped the moisture from her eyes, and tried to ignore the stitch that had crept into her side. "Surviving is easier than living."

"But it can be less rewarding." He had turned serious again.

Melissa was brought back from the notion of idle chatter to the fact that Andrew was busy making a point.

"Melissa, without a battle to fight to make things simple, without a legendary journey to make across the world, that simplicity simply does not exist. Life is full of the small, banal, trivial little chores that we face each day, and they normally add up to a whole lot of stress as we try to accomplish them. But when we do, when we stick it all out and look back, even when we know that we have to do it *all,* all over again, the accomplishment is no less meaningful than if we had travelled the long, arduous miles."

"How do we do it, though? How do we make those everyday things mean as much?"

Andrew smiled, his eyes twinkling behind his glasses. "By enjoying the things that we do. When people can only see the big fights, they miss out on the rest. They can't sit down at the end of a long trek with a book and a drink. They can't relax in a bath, or—"

"Or just sit and watch the stars." Melissa finished with a smile.

"Exactly. They have to ignore the trivial little joys as well as being able to ignore the trivial little chores."

"Balance."

"Balance, exactly so. And you won't find that balance in your box of memories, Melissa. You *can't* find balance in there. Because the *child* that those memories belonged to did not need the balance. She was too busy surviving. You're not the same person as she was, Melissa. None of us are the same people we started out as."

"And there's no way to find her again?" She was disturbed at how easy it was to talk about the girl she had once been as a separate person.

There wasn't a trace of laughter in him anymore. "Melissa, would you really *want* to?"

She looked at him and found that she had no answer to give.

The television showed the science-fiction programme and Melissa looked at it spasmodically – it was proving a good distraction.

Andrew had been right, of course. It hadn't been the memories of Lauren that she had wanted to find. The soft jumper that still held her little sister's scent, the small purple teddy bear, and the other odds and ends that had belonged to the eight-year-old remained in the box and to one side. On the floor before her was an assortment of things that were about herself only.

Sipping her wine as often as she glanced at the TV, she looked through the scattered debris of her childhood. She saw the black lipstick and black nail polish, along with the thick, black wristband, that had been used during her eight month stint as a goth when she'd been fifteen. There was a school notebook that she had filled with small pen-sketched doodles that she had intended at the time to be used as tattoo designs. There was a guitar-pick that she had been given by her school-boyfriend, a guitar-mad band-wannabe who was actually one of the decent types. There was the pair of old reading glasses that she'd had to wear; an old necklace; more school books, those containing goodbye messages from her school friends, filled in on the last day after exams. There were small stones and coins, and a dozen other small little things that she couldn't even remember why they had been important enough at the time to save.

As she picked up a programme from a concert that she had attended with a girlfriend and her family, remembering vaguely how much fun they'd had, another leaflet slipped out from inside it. Picking up her wine again with her left hand, she picked up the leaflet with her right, turning it the right way up so she could see it clearer.

Crowning the top of the leaflet, was the name of the place: Lunar Sanctuary. The photo on the front of it, beneath those silver words, was of a small pack of timber wolves, the one in front actually turned to look perfectly, straight into the camera. Melissa stared at the wolf, wishing that the picture had been taken in a close-up; she wanted to see its eyes.

Beneath the picture was the address of the wolf sanctuary, a small, basic map beneath showing the exact location. Melissa felt suddenly focussed, a tingling in the pit of her stomach as she read through the rest of the leaflet, taking in the details of the layout.

Frowning, she played everything over in her mind, for a moment wondering why she had put the leaflet for the sanctuary in the box and just forgotten all about it. She stared at the TV, looking past the pictures, as she drank her wine. She drank and wondered if the sanctuary could still be there.

When she realised that simply wondering wasn't going to provide her with any answers, Melissa drained her glass and went over to the computer. She looked out at the sky, burdened with dark clouds, while the computer booted up and the internet connected. Slowly, she typed into the search engine 'wolf sanctuary' followed by the location as it said on the map, then clicked search. Instantly it came back with a list of possible websites, but she ignored all but one, the top of the list. Excitement tingled through her as she read through the information of the place that did still exist, looking longingly at the pictures of the enclosures.

Smiling, she wrote down the phone number (that, at least, had changed since the leaflet had been printed), and switched off her computer. It was too late to call now, but maybe she'd ring up tomorrow, find out a bit more.

Standing up from the computer desk, she looked back at the

assorted jumble of items that she'd taken out of the box, child's possessions, and realised that she finally had an answer to Andrew's question.

* * *

Melissa switched off the engine and sat there, looking across the car park at the building on the other side, watching people walking towards it. She looked at the sign across the front of the building, seeing the name of the company she now worked for.

How could she possibly have thought that the *interview* was nerve-wracking?! She felt absolutely terrified at the prospect of going in! She closed her eyes and took a single deep breath, getting out of the car immediately after. She knew that if she sat there for much longer she would never get out, so she pulled herself up straight, put her handbag on her shoulder and walked to the door of her place of work.

As she'd promised to be, Lisa stood just inside the small enclosed lobby, waiting for her.

"Hi, Lisa."

"Hi, Melissa. You all ready?"

"In a nervous kind of way, yes."

Lisa laughed. "Come on. I'll take you through."

They walked to the only other door in the small lobby, and Melissa watched as Lisa used her small photo-ID badge to open the door. As she swiped through the box by the door, a red light disappearing to be replaced by a green on, a beep accompanying the change.

They walked through the door, and started along a corridor. "And here's yours," Lisa said, handing Melissa's own ID over.

Melissa looked down at the photo on it and grimaced slightly. "This is worse than the picture on my driving licence."

"You should've seen mine when I first started here. I had a perm!"

They laughed as they came to a room on the left, that Melissa had already been shown before; this time it was different, though – there were other people starting to sit down at the short rows of booths that housed computer desks, some looking at her with gentle curiosity.

"Okay," Lisa said, leading Melissa into the room and to a desk at the end of the back wall. "This is your desk, Melissa. No one else will be using it, so you can have a few personal bits and pieces around, although we ask that you don't clutter it up too much – it proves a distraction, otherwise."

Melissa nodded. She'd seen a couple of the desks with photos housed there, a couple with little figures. She doubted if she'd be bringing anything like that along; except, perhaps, a photo of Lauren.

"And, I showed you where the toilets and the canteen were last time, didn't I?"

"Yeah. Yeah, I know where they are."

Another woman with soft wavy ginger hair stood beside them.

"Melissa, this is Aimee Woods."

"Hi, Melissa." She stuck her hand out, which Melissa shook.

"Hi."

"Aimee's your team leader. She'll be the one keeping you busy while you're here."

"Busy, but not in a slave-labour kind of way." Aimee smiled pleasantly.

"Anyway, any problems, Aimee's the one to go to. She'll help you with anything you need. Right, well, I'll leave you to get settled in."

"Okay. Thanks, Lisa."

Aimee looked at Melissa warmly. "Did Lisa tell you that this week you'll just be familiarising yourself and training up on the software, and all that sort of stuff?"

"Yeah, she talked me through it all."

"Good. Well, have a seat."

When Aimee turned to grab a spare, nearby chair to bring beside hers, Melissa sat in the chair, *her* chair, that was already at the desk – *her* desk! – feeling truly happy to be where she was.

"I've just got to get everyone else started with their work, then I'll be back over, okay?"

"Okay." She watched as Aimee started to make her way around the room.

"First day?"

Melissa looked at the girl who had taken a seat at the desk next to hers, noting that she was maybe a couple of years older than herself, with short natural soft-blonde hair. "Do I look that nervous."

"It's a small place," the girl said. "You get to know everyone quickly."

"I'm Melissa."

"I'm Jan. Well, welcome to the mad house." She laughed, joined in by a couple of people on the surrounding desks.

Laughing as well, Melissa looked at her with interest. "If it's a mad house, I'll fit right in."

"Everyone here's mad, me more than anyone!" Jan's eyes twinkled, and she added a wink. "No, it's a good place to work. Everyone's really nice, and things are really relaxed. They don't mind you having a laugh and a joke around, just as long as you do the work."

Melissa looked around her, amazed at the difference from the place she had worked at last. There, it had been organised to a state of precision. People walked in and seemed to lose their sense of humour in the instant their feet crossed the threshold, the rooms immediately filled with the sounds of working and the odd whispered conversation – and that was only when it concerned work. It had been a nice place to work, but it had been stressful. *Very* stressful. It was totally different here. Already she could hear fingers tapping away at keyboards, but that was underneath the general chatter as they enquired as to each other's weekends. Melissa grinned as she saw that Aimee seemed to be the instigator of most of the conversations.

She could see herself being really happy here.

Chapter Fifteen

The three shining weeks of summer that had briefly lit the UK with its warmth in the middle of July was now a distant memory. The eighteenth of August was the same as it had been since those short-lived warm days had passed; unseasonably cold, cloudy and feeling too much like an over-enthusiastic seasonal-shepherd was herding winter in.

Michael for one was glad of the dip in temperature. It meant that he didn't roast as he sat in the car for hours, although as it darkened he did always need to put his coat on when it got just that little too cold.

Unbelievably, it had been almost five months since he had lost control – and briefly lost his sense of self-preservation – and stabbed Melissa's tyres. The very concise instructions that he had received from the police after that, even thought they had had no way to prove that it had been him, had scared him. They had made it very clear what consequences could follow if he continued, coming borderline to threatening him with charges if he didn't stop 'harassing' her. After that, he had learnt his lesson; he stopped being so obvious.

He learnt her new routine very quickly – it was fairly basic, after all: Monday, Tuesday and Thursday, work; her shrink on Wednesday morning, normally followed by a trip to the supermarket. Occasionally, she had gone out with the giggling-group of women from the place where she worked, but that didn't seem to happen very often.

He didn't follow her all of the time, didn't need to with her routine being as consistent as it was. But whenever he wasn't working he liked to be where she was, and even when he wasn't, he was thinking about being near her. Especially on Sunday evenings, like tonight. He would roll up to the house when it started to get dark, when he knew that the lights would be on and the curtains closed. Then he'd draw closer, and just sit and watch the house, waiting for the windows to darken as she went to bed.

This last week, though, he'd needed to be near her more. He had waited for her after work on Monday, watching as she left the building with the usual group. As she had started walking across the car park, Michael had straightened up in his car, ready to follow when she started driving away. Dismayed, and more than a little angry, he watched as the entire group of six had walked through the rows of the parked cars without stopping. They crossed the semi-busy road and went into the pub opposite.

Scowling, he locked up his car and followed them in. The bar was split into two sections, the bar running through the middle in between the two. Michael saw which side the group that contained Melissa stood, and went to the other side. He stood, drinking a glass of cola, and watching them.

Hearing them laughing and joking got too much, seeing Melissa with the three other woman and two men and enjoying herself *without him,* made him slam his glass angrily down on the bar and storm out. He drove away quickly, the blood pumping through his temples.

He'd called in sick to work the next day, claiming that a stomach bug had him confined to his bed. His boss had accepted it, actually slightly relieved that Michael wasn't going in; his temper had started to get a lot worse of late, and the fuse a hell of a lot shorter.

Following Melissa for the rest of the week was a little less stressful – she was just back to work, the psychiatrist, shopping and, most of all, staying at home.

When he got to her house on Friday night, close to midnight, he stopped at the start of the drive. Parked alongside her own little car were two others, and a lot of the lights were on in the house. On instinct, he killed his headlights, plunging the driveway back into darkness apart from the light that filtered through from the windows.

He left the car and walked up to the house, keeping his eyes on the front door so that he could be sure it didn't open without him knowing; he didn't want anyone to catch him sneaking around.

As he drew closer he could hear the alcohol-induced laughter of half a dozen women over the music that played over Melissa's CD player. He was angry, as he always was when he was close to Melissa, but at least there was no sign of any men being around – that would have been the last thing he could cope with. He'd stayed for only a few minutes before leaving; they sounded like they were set for the party to keep going through the night.

Following Melissa around the large shopping centre on Saturday afternoon wasn't the most thrilling time of his life, either, but that didn't make him walk away. And he had to wonder, while two aisles away and staring at her back, who she was thinking of while she looked at the low-cut tops she picked up to buy.

He stayed sitting where he was as he now watched the lights in the house in front of him turn off. Even with nothing to watch but the darkened building, it was another two hours before he finally left, only moments before Sunday night changed to Monday morning.

* * *

"No partying last week?"

Melissa grinned at the mischievousness of Andrew's tone. "No. No partying last week. I decided to give them a break from my undeniably animated personality! Think they deserve a rest!"

Andrew laughed. "You just don't want to end up with a hangover like the one you had the other weekend after they all stayed over!"

She groaned at the memory but still smiled. "God, I felt terrible! I really should have had more water that night!"

"Well, you know for next time."

"Yeah. Actually, Jan and Kelly wanted me to go out this weekend."

"Not interested in going?"

"I think I'm still adjusting to actually *having* friends again! I'm not used to socialising properly – it's been too long. It'll take me a while."

"Is that all it is?"

"That, and a weird week, this week."

"Yes. Big day tomorrow."

"Just a bit!"

"You working?"

Melissa shook her head. "I arranged with Aimee to work four days next week so I can take tomorrow off."

"Did you tell her why?"

"Yeah, she knows. A lot of them know."

Andrew smiled, and nodded towards her uncovered arms. "They're still a bit of a giveaway."

"It's strange," Melissa said, turning both of her arms over so that she could see the pale scars that ran along them. "You know, I hardly even see them anymore."

"They've faded a lot."

She looked at him and smiled. "You know that's not exactly what I meant."

"Yeah, I know."

"They're just not the first thing I notice about myself anymore; it's rare that they're consciously in my head."

"That's a good thing."

"That's a *very* good thing!"

"No one freaked out about them, at work?"

"Not really." She folded her arms again comfortable before her, but not in an attempt to hide the scars. "I mean, they were wary about mentioning it. I know that Kelly, especially, was worried about upsetting me. But when they knew I was okay about it, it stopped being an issue."

"Good. It sounds like you've made some really great friends."

"I have."

"So. Tomorrow's the fifth of September, Melissa."

"Really! I'd forgotten all about it, Andrew !" She grinned to show that she was just teasing.

"Well, that's why I thought I'd better mention it, just in case!"

"Yeah, right."

"Seriously, though. How are you feeling about it?"

Melissa sat on the chair, she had sat on once a fortnight for close to a year, and considered his question carefully. Andrew gave her the time, not inclined to rush her on a question this important.

After almost a minute of silence had moved by, Melissa finally answered. "I haven't got a clue how I feel about it, Andrew. I don't know how I'm *supposed* to feel about it."

"What's the first thing that comes to mind? Don't try and analyse it—"

"No, I let you do that."

"—just say what's going on in your head," he finished with a grin.

"Okay. I'm a little worried."

"Worried how?"

"Am I going to suddenly feel deeply depressed again? Is it going to be like a magic spell or something; the second it moves past midnight, am I going to be overwhelmed by sadness and despair?"

"Are you?"

"No." Melissa replied straight away. "But the worry of that possibility won't quite leave."

"That's understandable. What else?"

"I'm also worried that it'll just feel like any other day."

"That it won't feel special or important in any way?"

"Exactly. I want it to mean *something*. I don't want to be upset, or feel like I'm getting depressed again; but I would rather feel a little of that than feel nothing at all."

"Fire rather than smoke."

She laughed as he made the reference to her poems. "Yeah. I'm also excited."

"Excited?"

She sighed, but Andrew could see the smallest spark of elation in her eyes. "Because tomorrow, I'll have lasted a whole year! When I woke up in the hospital afterwards, when things started getting clearer in my head, I couldn't see myself being able to get through a day. I couldn't see how it could be possible for me to keep going *every* day.

"And instead of just getting through, instead of just surviving, I'm in a place I never thought I could ever be in again! I'm working, I have good friends; I'm able to do the little things that turn surviving into living."

"Sounds perfect." Andrew said.

"Ain't no such thing!" She laughed. "It is still hard sometimes, but it makes the times when it's not, so much better because of it."

"You really have done amazingly well, Melissa."

"I owe a lot of it to you, though."

"*You* did it, Melissa. I just—"

"Enough of the false modesty crap, Andrew. I may have done it, but you've been there to push me when I've needed it. I may have made some progress without your help, but I wouldn't have gotten this far. So, just accept my thanks without arguing!"

Andrew laughed and threw his hands up in a mock surrender. "Okay, okay, I concede." His tone dropped the mocking. "With thanks."

The silence that followed was a little awkward and it was Andrew that broke it before it could grow any deeper. "You spending tomorrow alone?"

"Yes. Alone. I've decided not to plan anything. I'll just let the day go as it goes; see what I decide to do in the morning."

"You don't think you'll be visiting your mum or anything?"

How much that question would have to do with the dream she had the following night, the night of the anniversary of her suicide attempt, Melissa wasn't ever able to figure out.

The cautious expectancy followed her down the stairs, was with her while she drank the first coffee of the day. Bright, hot sunshine filled the room and she nearly closed the curtains before stopping herself, her fingers still grasping the material. There had been too few sunny days this summer and autumn. Now that another had finally decided to arrive she wasn't going to shut it out. She let go of the fabric and sat back onto her sofa.

After lunch that anticipation mingled with a slight air of disappointment. Whatever the world-changing revelation was that she was expecting was well past due! So far, the day was what she had feared it would be – just another day.

She treated herself to a pizza, absolutely no desire to cook herself anything, and sat on the sofa again with a new movie playing, eating her dinner and drinking the wine she had poured herself while the sun started setting.

She cleaned her kitchen as she did every night, and she stood just looking at the clutter-free surfaces hit by the red sun. In a daze, she walked over to the little radio that was also lit by that glow and switched it on. Soft, easy-listening music flowed out of it and she turned to stare at the kitchen.

Melissa could almost see that girl, a year younger than she was now, lying curled up on the tiled floor. The tiles beneath her bleeding wrists were pooled with blood, the knife used lying within reach, if reaching it had been desired. Melissa could see the girl's skin growing paler as the seconds passed, the blood that should have been filling it escaping from her body. That young and fragile-looking girl with her eyes closed, only waiting to die.

Melissa smiled as she realised that it wasn't just another day, after all; that revelation had finally hit. Just as the girl from her childhood no longer existed, neither did that weak and scared girl that lay dying in her own blood. That girl *had* died that night and Melissa was the one who had survived.

The wolf stood in front of the mirror, the reflection of the woods behind her showing the moonlit expanse. The wolf stood there panting, tongue lolling out as it attempted to cool down after its run.

As if seen through a heat shimmer, the images in the glass flickered and when they settled again it was Melissa who now looked into the glass and at her human reflection, the wolf side of her now long gone.

Melissa looked at herself carefully in the moonlight at her completely naked form. There wasn't a single scar on her body, not one sign of cuts made by knife or scissors. The skin that reflected back at her was smooth and unblemished, untouched by any blade. That she was waiting for something was a fact that she knew without knowing how, as was the knowledge that she would wait for a long time. Feeling the grass tickling her skin, she sat down on the ground, continuing to stare into the mirror.

Suddenly drowsy, she closed her eyes, feeling the breeze playing over her skin, cool in the warmth of the night. Time had no meaning but she felt the lengthy passing of it anyway while her eyes stayed closed.

"Melissa."

She opened her eyes. Where her reflection had been when her eyes had closed was now someone else. There was nothing to throw shadows over the man, yet shadows were all she could see. She could tell that he was male – his shape and build told her that much – but that was all she could see; shadow was all there was *to see. He sat, cross-legged as she was, the reflection no longer hers in the mirror that was now a window.*

"Do I know you?" She asked the shadow-man.

No answer.

She thought for a moment. "Are you me?"

A silvery laugh flittered through the air. "A very intelligent assumption, but no. No, I'm not a part of you, Melissa."

She thought again, still trying to make more things about him out, without success. "Does it matter who you are?"

"No."

"I've never had a dream like this before."

"You have. Just not that you remember."

*"*Why *am I having this dream?"*

"You think you've sorted out everything from your past; you think you've started moving on from everything."

"But I haven't?"

"No."

"What else is there?" Even as she asked, a tiny flicker occurred deep down. She thought she knew the answer after all.

"You need to learn to forgive."

"I've tried."

"I know."

Melissa looked down at the silver grass in front of her, wondering at its silky texture. For a dream, it felt a little too real. She brought her head back up. "And if I can't? If I can't forgive?"

His sigh sounded as musical as his laugh had. "If you can't, then you need to find a way to let go of it all somehow. If forgiveness is something that you just can't find, then you need to find a way to let go."

Melissa lay in her bed, the covers covering the lower half of her body, looking at the darkness, unable to get back to sleep.

* * *

"Hi, Mellie. What you doing here?" She lifted her almost-empty glass in Melissa's direction. "Wanna drink?"

"No, thanks, Mum. I'm not staying."

Samantha nodded, emptied her glass and staggered off to the kitchen, swaying dangerously close to the doorframe as she passed. "Wha' brought you 'ere, Mellie?"

Melissa closed her eyes. "I needed to speak to you, Mum." As painful as it was to see her mother in such a bad state, as bad as the flat looked again with empty bottles everywhere, it strengthened Melissa's resolve. This was what she had always known she would have to do in the end.

"'Bout what?" Her mother walked over to the sofa and flung herself on it, spilling a fair amount of the whiskey onto the cushions.

"To tell you that I won't be visiting again."

Something about the sentence struck Samantha as funny and she burst out into gales of drunken laughter.

"Mum!" Melissa's tone at least stopped her laughter, although it didn't take the smile away.

"So you changed your phone number, now you won't be coming here again?"

"Right."

Nothing from her mother. She just sat, grinning, and moving the glass to her lips.

"Aren't you even going to ask why?!"

"No."

Melissa saw something very much like fear behind the drunkenness as she looked at her mum. "I'm still going to tell you, Mum, whether you want to know or not. And you're going to listen; you owe me that much."

Samantha said nothing, reverting to her silence, staring into the not-so-deep depths of the drink that still remained in her glass. But Melissa thought she was listening.

It was time to say all the things that she had kept bottled up. "You allowed him to, Mum. Everything Dad did to me, to Lauren, you let him do. You could have stopped him. You could have kept us safe. But you wouldn't. It was easier for you to pretend it wasn't happening, to lose yourself in *that* stuff –" she pointed at the glass – "then it would have been to keep your daughters safe. And you warned him, Mum. When people found out, you actually *warned* him. And you pretended that you hadn't known, but you did. All of it, you knew."

Still nothing from the woman on the sofa, except for that stolid silence.

"And I tried to understand; and when I couldn't understand, I tried to forgive you, but I can't do that, either. And now, all I can do is walk away from you, Mum, because me staying around isn't helping me. Because I'm waiting for you to admit it; I keep waiting for you to admit it and say sorry for letting it all happen. But I know that you won't."

Amazed that she had managed to keep her tone even, Melissa walked over to her mum, and kissed her softly on the cheek. "Goodbye, Mum."

The keys that she had taken form her key ring clattered slightly as Melissa placed them on the table as she passed. When that door closed behind her, Melissa felt ten years of heavy burden fall from her.

In the flat, Samantha Adams simply drained her glass once more before journeying to the kitchen for another refill.

Chapter Sixteen

"You flaming, stupid, bloody thing!" Melissa shouted her words out into the music-filled living room. She had a sudden image of herself as a child of about four or five, stamping her feet and throwing a tantrum, red-faced from screaming. She surprised herself into laughter with that image, and lost some of her agitation.

Before her annoyance could grow again, she picked up the leaflet and looked through it, trying to work out exactly where she had gone wrong. She read each step, her fingers playing gently over her lips as she did, lost in concentration. She could not see where she'd gone wrong. Still holding the paper manual in one hand, she picked up the satellite navigation system up and tried again, following each instruction carefully.

After three more attempts, she conceded defeat and put it down on the table beside her, fighting the urge to throw it across the room, but still with a smile. "Okay, I'll take the hint. I'll do it the old-fashioned way."

Grabbing her car keys from the kitchen, she darted quickly outside and brought her large map back into the house. With a steaming hot coffee in hand, she looked through the index until she found the place that she was looking for. Jotting down the road names and full directions on a small pad that she would take with her tomorrow, she worked out the best route.

It had been a good day at work, mainly because she'd been building up with excitement at the prospect of her little trip. Her colleagues, especially Jen, were amused by her excitement by the approaching treat; but, at the same time, they understood completely. It was just another reason that she loved her new friends.

She had rung the Lunar Sanctuary after work on the third of June and had been a little disappointed to find that it had changed slightly. According to the leaflet that she had for so many years, there were days every week when non-members were able to walk around the enclosure and spend time with the small number of wolves that had been raised with people. Because the sanctuary received no funding apart from the regular income from its members, now it was *only* its members who had that wonderful privilege. After thinking about it for about a week, and with a little gentle coercion from Jen, Melissa decided that it was more than worth joining. Tomorrow, she would be able to be close to the wolves, close enough to touch them.

She put the map and directions on the table, a small leather bound notebook that she used to jot down poem ideas (in case of inspiration from the magical, majestic creatures), and she placed her satnav and her car keys on top of them – that way she was guaranteed not to forget any of them. She stood in front of the table, her hand still lying on the top of her pile of things, and felt herself drifting.

Everything slipped just that little bit out of focus, things turned to smoke for just a second, and she simply stood, unable to think. Her eyes dropped close and she fought to shake off that sense of nothingness. When her eyes opened again, that sense left with the tinted-darkness and she turned to look outside.

The sun had started its descent and colours painted over the garden. As she stood there, a thin wisp of that smoke returning, she needed to be outside. Desire didn't come close to describing it; it was need, pure essential necessity. She was dehydrating, close to collapse, and outside was the water that would save her life.

She laughed. "The over-dramatic mental-blathering of the artistic!"

But it didn't change how true that analogy was to her, didn't change the exigency. She slipped her trainers on and walked outside.

It was probably a delayed reaction from her recent

anniversary, but she found herself walking away from the house, away from the direction of the main road, and towards the setting sun. She followed the path that she had taken before, this time walking instead of running and with no bandages covering her arms. The reflection that she had expected on the fifth, the contemplation that had appeared as a revelation, now came to her in the way that she'd anticipated.

This was the moment of perspective, this simple time of walking in the autumn warmth without anything hiding her scars. Just walking through fields that she had once run over, filled with contentment instead of pain and anguish. There was a peace in her that she was beginning to grow accustomed to, that was starting to become her normal state of being; and times like these helped bring it back to the front of her mind. And she knew that she needed to keep doing it, she needed to keep reminding herself of the wonder that had given the strength to fight. She didn't want the world to become mundane now that it had stopped hurting.

Walking took a lot longer than running had, and by the time she reached the place she was heading to, the world around her was completely drenched in reds, the recently cut wheat stalks crunching under foot. A part of her, the residue of the girl who had been in so much pain, tried to tell her as she looked around that the world was covered in blood; the stronger woman that she had become told her that the world was burning, that the reds and oranges that covered everything was passionate fire taking over.

Still moving, she rolled her eyes at herself, chortling. "I think I think too much." Realising how funny that was, she laughed loudly.

Her feet stopped suddenly, her laughter cutting off at the same time. There was no way she could know, there was no way that she could be so certain, not in the midst of all of the identical fields; yet she was. With the burning setting sun, Melissa stood in the place, in the exact spot, where she had fallen to her knees as she had beseeched the moon. She could feel how she had felt, the agony that had filled her. She tasted it with her eyes closed, feeling the latent energy that she had left in this place, wondering exactly what had caused her to walk this path again.

Where she had knelt, pleading for a chance, she lowered herself and sat cross-legged, looking at the deepening sky. She absorbed the warmth on her face, and took everything in; it just felt right, just sitting and taking in the beautiful sunset!

It also felt almost as if she were watching her last ever sunset; that something was close to ending.

* * *

It was boiling in his mind, in his body, that anger that was building constantly, every day. It was past eleven o'clock, and her car was not there! He had walked around the car park, looking at each vehicle that was parked there, scrutinising each new car as it drove in. But the car park at the mental health clinic did not contain her car. Where the *hell* was she?

He started his own car up, but left the handbrake on, his hands gripping the wheel. His knuckles were white from the pressure, his eyes closed, as he breathed in the anger. The horn screamed out briefly as he hit the centre of the wheel. Still furious at the wasted time, at her being anywhere except where she was supposed to be, Michael made the tyres squeal as he sped away, heading to her house.

The car wasn't there, either. There was no sign of her. He walked around the front of the house, peering into the windows and seeing nothing. He scrambled over the back fence, jumping down and nearly twisting his ankle as he hit the ground. A thin small pain went through his hand, and he looked to see the blood seeping slowly from the graze on his knuckles.

He stomped to the kitchen window and cupped his hands so

he could peer in without the light affecting the view. He saw her coffee cup on the counter, beside the sink, next to the bowl she had used for her breakfast. From the living room window he saw the normal tidy room, except for a couple of things on the dining table.

It was ridiculously stupid, and he knew it was. He was letting his temper control him, and it really was an idiotic thing to do, but still he moved back to the back door. Looking through, he could see her spare keys where she always kept them, but there was no way he could reach them even if he were to break the window.

"Now, there's an idea," he whispered, grinning.

Turning around, he scanned the ground around him, but could see nothing that he could use. Sliding the bolt to open it, Michael used the gate to leave and went out to his car. In the boot, amongst the tools in the toolbox, he found a hammer and took it back with him.

The windows were strong; he had to admit that. It took six very heavy hits for the living room window to crack, and another three to force out enough glass for him to be able to get through without slashing his skin. He took her black wheelie bin over from its position near the corner of the fence, and tipped it over. The lid opened, spilling out carrier bags, their handles tied to keep the rubbish inside. He stood on the bin and boosted himself up, still managing to catch the palms of his hands on small loose shards of glass.

The first thing that Michael saw was the painting on the wall. He wanted to rip it down, to stand on it, break it, smash it to pieces. Whether he would have done it or not, Michael never found out. As he walked towards the sofa, perhaps to take down the picture that hung on the wall behind it, he glanced at the pieces of paper on the surface of the table, and stopped.

He ignored the address book and picked up the leaflet.

"Lunar Sanctuary?" He read the address, trying to figure out exactly where the place was. After all, it was worth a look. Melissa couldn't stop smiling. She was in complete awe of where she was, of what she was near.

When she'd arrived, parking in the small gravel car park, she'd walked to the visitor's centre with her notebook and pen in hand, gazing at the surrounding forests. Clouds were passing in front of the sun, giving her occasional shelter from the heat, helped along by the cool breeze. Her feet crunching over the small stones, she breathed in the scents of the air around her, the freshness of it all, thinking about the wonder of synchronicity. What were the chances of her day off from work coinciding with an available day to visit the sanctuary *and* on the day of the full moon?

The two women turned and smiled at her as she walked into the combined visitors centre and shop, on the outside of the main enclosure. They were both dressed in jeans and loose T-shirts, the one in her mid-forties with her shortish hair pulled back in a ponytail, and the younger one with her shoulder-length hair resting easily against her neck.

"Melissa?"

Melissa looked at the one with the ponytail as she approached. "Yeah, that's me."

"Welcome to the Lunar Sanctuary. I'm Trish, we spoke on the phone, and this is Caitlin."

"Hi."

Trish looked at the almost awe-struck look on Melissa's face, one that she was used to seeing on the faces of people who came to the sanctuary; and one that she felt on her own face most times. "You about ready for this?"

"More than ready."

"Come on, then."

Melissa followed them to the back of the centre, looking at the many leaflets and souvenirs; the mugs, the T-shirts, the key rings, and the many other knickknacks that were all decorated with images of wolves. She was very glad that she'd brought some money with her.

She walked outside again, back into the sunlight, and stopped, momentarily stunned. She didn't see the knowing look that passed between the two women. She saw only the view before her.

The high chain-link fence that ran around the outside of the sanctuary stretched for so far that Melissa couldn't see the other side. The land before her dipped slightly into a tree-filled valley, and she could see another, smaller – but perhaps over two acres square – enclosure. Amongst the clumps of trees in that inner enclosure, Melissa saw movement.

"Wow." It was more of a sigh than an actual spoken word.

"It's impressive," Caitlin said.

Melissa turned and smiled. "How do you get used to working here? I'd be so mesmerised that I wouldn't actually be able to do anything."

"Trust me; that happens sometimes."

"I'll bet. I just—" Melissa's mouth continued to hang open as she stopped mid-sentence.

Walking along a path towards them, held loosely on leads by a woman and a man, both who looked to be in their late fifties, were two of the animals she had come to see. Even from the short distance, the timber wolves were clearly larger than domestic dogs. The one leading the woman had a very light brown coat, speckled with grey, while the other's fur was a deep rich brown.

"Oh, God."

Trish had sidled up beside her and spoke quietly, laughter clear in her voice. "This is the part I like the most, Melissa. Seeing people's reactions when they first see them."

"It's just... I can't..." She laughed. "I can't describe how incredible it feels, seeing them walking *towards* me." That was an understatement. Her heart was pounding quickly beneath her breast, and she could feel the blood burning as it ran through her veins. As beautiful and awe-inspiring as the scenery around her was, it was trite and meaningless in comparison to the captivating graceful creatures that were drawing closer.

"And they're the domesticated wolves? The ones hand-reared?" She laughed again, shaking her head, before immediately answering her own question. "Course they are, seeing as though they're on leads. Sorry."

"It's okay." Trish grinned. "Yeah, they've been with us since being born. The paler one is Diana, and the darker one is Selene."

Although she hadn't felt as she had been breathing since the appearance of the wolves, she now felt what breath she had being stolen from her. "Diana and Selene?" She looked at Trish in wonder.

"You know why those names?"

She nodded, still feeling swept away. "They're goddesses. Goddess of the Moon." Melissa turned her attention back to the animals named after goddesses that she, herself, had prayed to.

"I'm impressed. Not many people know that," Caitlin said from behind them.

"Well, I think," said Trish as she looked at the pendant that lay against Melissa's chest, "That she may have reason to. You're a pagan, yeah?"

"That's right." The defences that had started to build disappeared at the lack of hostility in Trish's sparkling brown eyes.

"Cool."

"How'd you know?"

"My brother-in-law's a pagan. Fully practicing witch. I recognised the symbol on your pendant."

Melissa nodded, smiling, and turned back to the approaching wolves.

"You remember what I said over the phone?"

"Yes. Let them come to me; I'm not to go to them. Don't try and dominate them, let them make all the moves."

"And remember how strong they are. They're much, much

stronger than domestic dogs."

Melissa giggled. "They're definitely not poodles or springer spaniels."

Trish laughed, joined by Caitlin. "That's a safe bet!"

"Hi," the woman who walked with Diana called.

"Hi," Melissa said to both of the handlers.

"Okay, Melissa," Trish said, gently placing a hand on her arm. "Just like we talked about."

"I feel really nervous."

"You don't have to do this."

She grinned wildly. "Nothing could stop me. It's a good nervous."

Trish grinned back and nodded.

Melissa turned her face back to the wolves that drew slowly nearer and, with Trish and Caitlin both doing the same, Melissa sank to her knees, sitting with her buttocks resting on the back of her legs and looked at the wolves. Both of the handlers had stopped moving; the two she-wolves were now stepping towards her with no restraints, their leads dragging on the ground behind them.

Her heart felt as if it was going to leap out of her chest through her mouth, and she could feel sweat beading onto her forehead and the palms of her hands. Diana, the lighter wolf, moved to Melissa's left, going to Caitlin, tongue lolling out and tail wagging; Selene went the other way, to Trish's side. As the two women who jointly ran the sanctuary stroked the animals that had gone to them, Melissa could smell them, and closed her eyes to take it in.

She nearly screamed as a wet nose nuzzled against her bare arm, and barely bit down quick enough to stop herself from letting it out. She opened her eyes and looked at Selene's fur. She was so close that it tickled at Melissa's skin and she was able to see the minute details that made up the different shades of her luscious, thick coat. When the animal leant against her, nuzzling against her face and almost pushing her over, Melissa realised just *how* strong the creatures were, but she sensed no danger from the docile animal. Smiling, she allowed the wolf to sniff at her face and slowly, Melissa lifted her left arm, planting her right one on the ground to stop herself from toppling backwards, and moved it over the surface of the fur, her fingers sinking into the softness.

There was nothing that could have made her feel more fulfilled and complete.

Michael had programmed the address of the wolf sanctuary into his own satnav, and had started out almost straight away. Almost two hours later, he arrived at the sanctuary. It had taken him a little longer than the satnav had advised him; but that was mainly because he'd stopped at a shop to pick up some food. The carrier bag that contained the ready-made sandwich, crisps, chocolate bars, and cans of cola was sitting in the passenger footwell.

Straight away, he was able to see Melissa's little red car in the gravel-filled car park. He was able to see it immediately because it was so small, and there were only six cars in total parked there. It complicated things: it meant that, if he were to park there as well, she would see his car – and him – at once.

He tapped his finger on the steering wheel, thinking, trying to find the best solution. He did the only thing he could think of. He turned around and left the sanctuary car park, heading back the way he'd come. At the lay-by, he pulled in and switched off the engine. He turned his rear-view mirror slightly so that it showed him the road behind him clearly, picked up the bag and started to dig in. He slumped down in his seat a little, getting comfortable and settling himself in to wait.

She was still buzzing, still able to smell them, even with them nowhere near. They'd walked around the whole sanctuary, seeing the other small inner-enclosure that Melissa had missed in the overall view that she'd had. Because they had had to be completely hand-reared, completely domesticated and used to humans, they couldn't be integrated into the pack that roamed in the inner enclosure that Melissa had seen. They had walked for hours around the place, with Selene and Diana leading the way, once again held by their handlers, and the afternoon started to grow later.

Now, she sat on the grass with her notebook and pen on her lap, looking into the darkness of the forests within the enclosure she had spied from the top of the small valley. Somewhere in the shadows, hidden within the trees, was a pack of the most majestic animals in the world. Although she had glimpsed them moving, little flashes of moving colour, she hadn't seen any clearly; but maybe it was enough, just those little glances.

She looked at sky, at the sun that had started to move downwards, and felt a little bit of disappointment. The sanctuary would be closing soon; Trish had told her that it would be closing before dark, but that she would have until then to sit and watch the enclosure for sign of them. Melissa knew that wolves were private animals, quite shy by nature, but still – there was that small disappointment.

She stood, and stretched her legs a little, getting ready to trek back to the centre (and the shop!), and looked back into the enclosure.

Out of the darker shadows, but still shaded from the setting sun, stood a single wolf, looking directly at her.

On legs that didn't feel completely steady, she took a couple more steps towards the fence, mindful of the rules not to get too close. With a clear metre between her and the chain-link boundary she looked at the creature that looked back at her with interest.

Tears filled her eyes, running down her cheeks, and a lump formed in her throat. Her stomach tightened and her heart fluttered. Her legs lost their strength and she collapsed back onto the ground, aware of the pain that jolted through her but not feeling it. She was sobbing, unable to catch her breath.

She saw her dream, the reflection-dream, when her wolf-self had shimmered into her human-self, that dream that had been sparked by her anniversary. She saw the image of the wolf that she had been, glimpsed for a moment in that inexplicable mirror. She saw that wolf, the markings on the fur, the differences in the colours.

And she looked before her, at the wolf that stood in the enclosure and stared back, and saw those markings, reversed now that they weren't seen through a reflection.

The wolf in front of her lifted its muzzle and howled into the sky, and Melissa's heart broke at its sound. Her hand covered her mouth to stifle the sobs as that sound suffused her soul with its wonderful sadness.

A voice that had never had any physical sound, that had only ever been heard as a whisper in the wind, was brought back to her in memory.

Listen to the call of your spirit guide to lead your way. Follow the call and the passions of the wolf.

Even when the wolf's howl had ended, Melissa found that she could still hear it resounding in her head.

Each time a car appeared in the mirror, Michael's attention snapped back into red-alert. With the sun starting to get lower, it was harder to see even the colour of the approaching cars until they were almost driving past, the reflecting light making the metal shine too brightly for him to be able to see. But he didn't grow lax, didn't become dulled by the non-appearance of Melissa's car. Even while urinating out of the open passenger-side door, he was aware of the car – a light blue five-door estate – that passed him by.

The hours passed and he sat in silence, simply watching the cars that drove along the quiet road. He really had no idea why he'd become so obsessed with her; why he was sitting and waiting; no idea why he had broken into her house. He also had no idea what he was going to do when he finally *did* see her car approaching. All he knew was that she hadn't been where she was supposed to be, had started doing things outside of her standard routine, and it made him angry.

So, he waited.

She sat in her car for a very long time before starting it up. The tears had dried and the salty tracks that they had left had been washed away. She was still haunted by that sound, it echoed deep inside her, and the world had fallen distant. It wasn't the same as she normally felt, it wasn't a world made of smoke; things around her were still there, still solid, but they were being viewed through a thin veil, just one layer separating Melissa from what surrounded her.

She pulled herself up straighter in her seat, rearranging her seatbelt so that it sat more comfortably over her chest, and consciously forced the veil to part, to move aside so that she could at least focus on driving. She took the satnav out of the glove box and popped it into place, turning it on purely out of habit.

The bag of souvenirs nearly slipped off the seat next to her as she started the car rolling, but she was able to grab hold of them. Leaning backwards, she put them on the floor behind the passenger seat, wedging them in a little to stop them moving around.

As she stopped at the exit, Melissa felt a sudden impulse to turn right instead of left. Turning right would take her further away from her home – she wasn't even sure what was in that direction without consulting her map. Yet still, some part of her wanted to turn that way.

In the back of her mind, she heard the memory of that howl and, incredible as it seemed, it appeared to be coming from the left, from the route that would take her home. She sat there, undecided, for two minutes, feeling herself split in half, compelled in different ways to take different directions. Remembering the words of that silver-toned voice, she turned towards home, letting the howl lead her.

She drove along, lost in the strangeness that had been invocated by that wolf-call, and although she saw the car in the lay-by, she didn't really *see* it. She drove on, oblivious to the car that pulled out quickly and started to follow her.

He wasn't able to see the car in any detail until it was almost alongside. The second he saw the Melissa was driving, he started the engine and pulled out behind her, fastening his seatbelt as he drove. He left a little bit of distance between them; he didn't want her to see it was him just because she happened to glance up. He could feel the adrenalin building up in him, and still didn't know what he was doing.

Almost half way home, Melissa was pleased at how well she was remembering the directions without having to look at the notepad that she'd written them down in. She was able to follow the signs around her, choosing the right paths even though she was still completely absorbed in the wondrous and peculiar day she was still having.

The quiet, tree-lined road started to open a little, the trees dispersed with the occasional building, and more cars started travelling in the opposite direction. She wondered, vaguely, why the car behind her was at such a constant distance, but thought nothing much of it.

She dropped her sun-visor to try and deflect the brilliant burning light of the descending sun so that she didn't have to squint any more. She glanced up to the car behind, its colour and design masked by the light bouncing off its bonnet, and it was still at its distance. Some warning tingled at the back of her neck as she watched other cars overtaking it when its speed didn't increase. Her eyes, mainly on the road in front of her, flickered regularly to her rear-view mirror. Although she wasn't certain, she thought that it had been following her since the sanctuary.

She was already travelling at the speed limit, her father's fatal misadventure having pounded the peril of dangerous driving into her at foundation level, but she increased her speed by five miles per hour, her eyes keeping a check on what was happening behind.

The two cars that had moved in between her and the one that had sent that warning through her, also increased their speed, but that other one remained at its previous pace.

Melissa laughed in nervous relief. "Getting paranoid, girl." The smile slipped away; that car had caught up again.

"Oh, God."

Panic was gnawing at her, deep in the pit of her rolling stomach, and her mind went blank, filled with terror. Her hands were sweating as she held the steering wheel, and the start of a headache began to throb at her temples. Looking at the car that had now matched speed so that the distance between them was back to what it had been, Melissa felt the urge to curl into a ball and hide. She caught sight of her eyes in the mirror, saw the startled deer-in-the-headlights expression, and felt angry with herself. With the palm of her hand she hit the edge of the steering wheel, which gave the same effect as being slapped in the face.

"Grow up and get a grip!" she yelled in the confines of her car. After all, she was only speculating about the car following her – her little test had hardly been conclusive. Nevertheless, her good rationale had banished the frightened feeling (most of it, anyway), and she leant over, keeping her eyes on the road ahead, rooting around in the glove box. She pulled at the hands-free kit that she kept in the car and, still being careful of what was going on as she drove, she plugged it into her phone which she left on her lap, and hooked the earpiece over her ear.

"Okay," she said, now feeling much better. "That's something, at least."

Two cars back, that car still followed.

When the two cars overtook him and occupied the space between Melissa and himself, his initial reaction was to speed up so that he could move directly behind her, but he realised that that would take him too close; far too close, and it would only be a matter of minutes before she saw who was behind her. So he held back, allowing the two cars to mask him from her view. They stayed in that pattern for a couple of miles, and then, for no reason, Melissa sped up.

Caution filtered into him. He was very aware of her rules about speeding; she had asked him a few times while they had been in the car together to slow down. So, there had to be a reason for the sudden change of speed.

Again, he held back, not wanting to confirm any suspicions she may have had, but as the space between them grew, he realised that he was going to have to catch up. He was simply going to have to hope that something else had caused her to break the speed limit.

Still following her directions, Melissa continued on her way home, manoeuvring around the third roundabout. She was now completely sure that the car was following her.

She was travelling along dual carriageways now, the speed of her own car held at a steady seventy miles per hour, yet lots of cars sped past her; but the blue car was not one of them. It remained behind her, still at its perfectly held distance. She had a hunch about who it was, who it *had* to be, but she was praying that she was wrong. If it was Michael, for him to have followed her as far as he had, she couldn't believe that it could be for anything good.

As the roads started to fill up, she broke her rule again, and sped up. It wasn't the smartest thing to do, she knew, but she had to know.

"What the fuck are you doing, Melissa?"

Michael watched as Melissa's speed increased rapidly, and she pulled out of the inside lane, overtaking cars that now slowed her down, moving out to the outside lane. With now twelve cars between them, Michael lost sight of her.

"Shit!"

He stamped his foot down and hurried to catch up, to close the gap that had materialised so suddenly and surprisingly. In the outside lane as she had been, he sped along, searching ahead for her car. He undertook a car, moving into the middle lane.

"Where are you, Melissa? Where the hell did you disapp—" He stopped, having glanced briefly to his left. "You sneaky bitch," he whispered.

In the inside lane again, looking directly back at him, Melissa stared out of her car.

"Oh, shit."

He had done what she had thought he would do, but she didn't feel better for being right. She had seen the total and complete fury on his face, that she had tricked him into revealing his presence.

She looked through the mirror and watched as he forced his way behind her, making the car that had been there to brake. The driver hit his horn, but Michael ignored it – he was concentrating solely on meeting her eyes in the mirror.

"Michael. What are you doing?" Despite the setting sun being in front of her, she flicked the rear-view mirror so that all she could see was a dark, phantom reflection of the view behind her, and picked up her phone. She didn't want to do it, but the worry inside her told her that she didn't have a choice. For the second time in life, little over a year since the first, Melissa was connected to the emergency services operator.

"Which service: police, fire or ambulance?"

"Police." Given the circumstances, Melissa didn't worry about appearing rude or blunt. And as a click came over the line, and a female voice replaced the male one almost instantly, she knew that pleasantries hadn't been expected.

"Police emergency. Can you give me your name and the number you're calling from?"

"I'm Melissa Adams. I'm on my mobile, I don't know the number."

The operator read out the number that had appeared on his screen. "Is that correct?"

"I guess so, yes."

"What's your emergency?"

"I'm driving, and someone's following me. An ex. He's had police warnings a couple of times to stay away from me. He's been violent before; he has a temper."

"You're worried about his intentions?"

"Yes."

"Okay, Melissa, do you know where you are?"

"Um…" Close to panic, Melissa looked at grass verges around the roads but could see no signs. She sighed in exasperation at herself. "Yeah, I've got my satnav on." Careful to keep watching the road, she glanced at the navigation system and gave the operator her location.

"Okay. Melissa, my name's Carol. I need you to stay on the line, okay?"

"Okay."

She looked into the mirror again, and saw Michael still behind.

Michael saw Melissa looking around, then looking at something in her car. He had the growing suspicion that maybe she was calling the police. It really should have concerned him, but he had a gut instinct that things were going to work out. He had an idea, finally, of where it was all heading. His anger had given him a clarity as to his intentions.

"Okay, Melissa, we've got some traffic officers on their way to you, just keep going straight, okay?"

"Okay."

"Is he still behind you?"

There was no reason for her to even bother looking – she could feel the intensity of his gaze. "He's still there."

"Are you still heading north?"

"Yeah. I'm about three hundred yards from the next slip road."

As the lane started to branch off, Melissa noticed Michael's car moving to overtake. He pulled alongside of her and looked over.

"He's gone next to me now."

"What's he doing, Melissa?"

"Nothing, just driving alongside."

"Okay. Well, just keep heading down this road. The officers will be with you soon, Melissa. You're okay."

"Okay. I just wish I knew—"

Melissa was shunted, her car shoved towards the slip road, Michael's car forcing her off the dual carriageway. "Shit!"

"Melissa? What's wrong? What was that noise, Melissa?"

Melissa struggled with the wheel, trying to turn back onto the road Michael had pushed her away from. "He's just hit the fucking car, sending me up the slip road!"

"Melissa, can you stay on the dual carriageway?"

"No. He's blocking me, I can't get back on."

"Melissa, don't panic. I can send the police car after you, they're not far away. Just stay calm. Now listen, I need you to keep talking to me, keep telling me what's happening."

Melissa was now back on a single-lane road, and Michael had

dropped back behind her. She kept her eyes firmly on the road that was unfolding before her.

"Melissa. I want you to try to keep to the main roads if you can. Try to keep to roads that have a lot of traffic on."

"Okay." She looked at the approaching roundabout. "There's a roundabout coming up." All three roads looked the same, and she had no idea where to go. "I'm going to go straight on."

"Straight on at the roundabout? Okay." The woman paused for a while. "Okay, Melissa. I've told the officer. Keep talking to me. You're doing really well."

The few cars that she had seen on the roads started to filter off, and Melissa looked at the surroundings that started to encompass her. "Oh, no."

"Melissa, what's wrong?"

Worry edged Carol's voice, and Melissa could feel panic biting at her again. "It's a B road." She looked at the dense woodland that had now started to overhang the road. "I've gone down a fucking back road!"

Melissa lurched forwards as Michael's car rammed her's.

PCs Bell and Patel raced along the road, looking for the junction they needed. PC Bell looked at the fast approaching sign. Taking his eyes off the road for a second, he looked at his colleague. "Danny, is this it?"

"I think so." He spoke into the phone that had been clamped to his ear since they'd had the incident details came through. "We're approaching a slip-road, junction number eight. Do we take this junction?" He listened for a second. "Yeah, down this one, mate."

"Right."

With the siren and lights going, the car slowed a little from its high speed as it started up the slip road, cars in front pulling over to one side to give them some room to go past.

Michael grinned viciously as he saw the road beginning to narrow, the edges of the woods beginning to encroach. As they travelled at just under sixty miles an hour, Michael thought he heard sirens in the distance.

He increased his own speed and hit the back of Melissa's car, watching as she reeled forwards. Her car started to veer towards the side, but she managed to correct it. He hit it again. This time, she wasn't able to hold it steady and the nose of the little red car turned towards the rising verge. He shot forwards again, using his car to ram hers into the sloping ground, lodging it firmly in place.

The seatbelt pulled tightly against her chest, and her neck felt like it had been knocked slightly out of joint, her shoulders aching.

"Melissa? Are you still there?"

"Yeah," she was able to gasp. "He's just pushed me into the verge." She looked at the little bit of smoke that was rising from under her bonnet. "Oh, God! My car's screwed!"

"Melissa, are you hurt?"

"No, I don't think so." She winced, however, as she turned around to face behind her, releasing her seatbelt from its clasp. "He's getting out of the car."

Carol's voice rose in pitch. "Melissa. They're going to be there so, so soon. You need to stay in the car. Do you hear me, Melissa? You need to stay in the car."

The gnawing creature of panic started running loose in her, and her hand fumbled for the door handle. "I can't! He's coming!"

"Melissa, you *need* to stay with me, here. Melissa—"

Melissa tried to grab the phone as it fell, tried to snag the wire of her hands-free kit as she stumbled out of the car, but it slipped from her fingertips. She couldn't spare the time to retrieve it, and just left it lying where it was.

He hadn't braced himself as well as he thought he had. He hit the side of his head on the rear-view mirror, knocking it from where it hung. A small trickle of blood ran down the side of his face and into his eye, and he wiped it away. His head felt dizzy, his eyes plagued by an invasion of dancing lights. He shook his head to clear it, regretting the movement instantly as a pain started to beat in the centre of his mind.

But he was smiling. Her tiny little car was blocked in, and he could see very little movement from in front of him. Michael moved his hand, released his seatbelt and started reaching for his door handle. For some reason, he was struggling to get a grip on it. He looked up and saw her staring, eyes wide and fearful, at his movements.

"No!" he shouted hoarsely as she started to get out of the car. As she started to scramble up the small embankment that her car had become embedded in, Michael pushed his weight against the stubborn door, pulling the handle. He spilled out, headfirst, onto the tarmac, pain again turning his mind red and incapable of thought. He made some grunting-type of scream and struggled to his hands and knees in time to see Melissa running into the trees.

PC Bell expertly pulled the car up beside the two crashed cars, while his colleague spoke over the phone.

"Confirmed RTC, approximately three miles from the roundabout."

The younger, but more experienced, officer was already out of the vehicle, rushing to the blue car. The door hung open and a splash of dark sticky liquid decorated the black tarmac. He looked into the red car, noting the dropped phone, and turned back to the other officer.

"Both empty."

Dan Patel reported the information back, informing them that they were proceeding on foot into the woods.

Over the earpieces, they heard the welcome news that other officers were heading to the scene.

As they both reached the top of the small but very steep incline, the descending sun filling the trees with burning light, they peered around, looking for any sign in the dense wood.

"Where do we—"

PC Patel's voice was cut off as a scream echoed to them. They raced off to the right as other sirens began to grow closer.

Melissa couldn't think as she ran deeper into the woods. She could hear him running behind her, gaining ground as she felt the muscles in her legs burning. She ran through the alternating bursts of reddened sunlight and dark, cool shadows.

Just as she thought her legs were going to give, she was hit in the back and fell forwards, her face crashing into the hard, stone covered ground. She rolled onto her side and looked up in time to see Michael pulling his leg back. She was looking into his face, at the furious but blank expression, as his foot shot forwards into her stomach. Her knees pulled into her chest as the breath left her, eyes creased closed. She lay there, gasping and fighting for air to find its way back into her lungs, unable to think. Her legs shot out before her as he kicked her again, this time in the centre of her back, blinding pain like nothing she had ever imagined shot through her, wiping everything else and turning the whole world white.

"You stupid bitch." He was leaning over her, his fists pummelling her stomach again and again.

In a distant way, Melissa thought about her lost phone, laying abandoned on the ground. She thought about the woman, Carol, who had tried to keep her safe, tried to keep her calm by promising the soon arrival of help.

How long had she been in the woods? Had those promised-helpers seen the collision yet? With the breath that she had, she was sobbing with each blow that hit her. She knew, from the stitch-like pain in her chest, that she wouldn't be capable of anything but gasping breaths soon. Fighting against the pulling tightness in her lungs, and the metallic taste of her own blood in the back of her throat and in her mouth, she pulled in all of the air she could.

Michael actually jumped backwards as she screamed into the air, the anger shocked out of him, but only for a moment. His fist feet slammed into her stomach again, harder, and the air was again pushed out.

She closed her eyes, feeling herself giving in.

The three officers who had also arrived had managed to catch up with them quickly, thanks to Patel's surprisingly accurate directions given over the radios, surprising because of the lack of noticeable landmarks within the woods, and all five of them raced over to the man who sat beside a gasping form, his fists hitting over and over.

Together, they hauled him off, and in almost choreographed movements turned him around and put him on the ground. While one of them held his head firmly to the ground, turned to the left to prevent smothering him, two held his legs securely, and Patel and Bell put cuffs onto his wrists. With him secured and held on the ground, not even struggling against them, PC Bell rushed to the girl, pushing the button on his radio.

"Charlie Hotel two-niner."

"Go ahead."

"Ambulance required. Female victim, multiple injuries to the face and body."

"Location?"

"South-west of the RTC, in the woods."

"Received. Ambulance on way."

He crouched beside the beaten woman, the short sleeve of his shirt rising a little more on his arm as he leant forwards. "What's your name, love?"

Melissa struggled to swallow down the blood that was pooling in her mouth, and she could feel some of it trickling over her lips as she answered. "Melissa Adams."

"Okay, Melissa. There's an ambulance on its way; they'll be here soon. I want you to stay as still as you can, until they get here. Okay?"

"Okay," she whispered.

He sat back a little and looked at the bruises that were brewing on her face, and the blood that covered her teeth. Behind him, he could hear one of his colleagues reading the attacker his rights as they all walked him back towards the cars.

"Can you open your eyes, Melissa? I don't want you drifting off or anything."

It was an effort, especially with one of her eyes starting to puff closed, but she was able to eventually, and looked upwards. In the gaps in the trees, directly above her, Melissa could see the rich sky. It was filled with dark reds and burnt oranges that streaked the clouds and made the leaves shine with firelight.

"When the fire's descent enflames the clouds and burns the skies," she whispered in a dazed voice, tears leaking from her eyes, that echo of the howl invading her heart again.

"What, Melissa? What did you say?" He moved closer, and Melissa's eyes found his, seeing the soft-hazel eyes behind the oval-rimmed glasses. She smiled, her forehead creasing. "I know you."

"You do?" PC Bell didn't know if she did or not; her face didn't look familiar, but with the injuries she had sustained it would have been hard to tell if he did know her. But he felt a strange prickling sensation at the back of his neck.

"Yeah." She started to look away, fighting a cough that wanted to erupt but not succeeding, hearing sirens of an approaching ambulance. She saw the mark on his arm, and moved her hand.

"Melissa?" He was worried by the distant look that was creeping into her eyes, and very glad that he could hear voices getting closer. "Don't try and move."

Despite the pain that started to wrack her body, she lifted his arm, turning it slightly so that she could see the picture. Where the scars were on the inside of her arm, on the inside of his was a tattoo, filled with colour and passion. She looked at the tattoo of the wolf's head, a full moon with drifting clouds behind it. She felt herself lost in its detailed and consuming yellow eyes.

When she looked up, the police officer was stunned to see the happiness in her green eyes as they met his. He watched her lips moving, straining to hear the words spoken in a whisper.

"Listen for its call. Listen for the call of your spirit guide to lead your way. When the fire's descent enflames the clouds and burns the skies; when the ground falls from beneath your feet, and the wolf stares back into your eyes, give yourself over. Listen to its call to find the one who also seeks you. Follow the call and the passions of the wolf."

Before he could ask her, he was moved aside, her hand falling from his arm.

He stood back and watched as the medics examined her, and helped them to place her gently onto the stretcher. He then watched as they took her through the woods, staring after her in uncertainty.

The man who had, three hundred and eighty-six days before and in a drunken despair, sent a song dedication over the radio, an anonymous dedication to all of those who were hurting, who were as lonely as he was, started to follow the medics. Marshall Bell walked through the woods and watched as the badly beaten girl with the strangely hopeful and contented green eyes was carried into the ambulance, feeling strangely hopeful himself.

Survive the bad, so you can live through the good
– Beth Murray, 26th August 2009

Lodestone Books is a new imprint, which offers a broad spectrum of subjects in YA/NA literature. Compelling reading, the Teen/Young/New Adult reader is sure to find something edgy, enticing and innovative. From dystopian societies, through a whole range of fantasy, horror, science fiction and paranormal fiction, all the way to the other end of the sphere, historical drama, steam-punk adventure, and everything in between. You'll find stories of crime, coming of age and contemporary romance. Whatever your preference you will discover it here.